Claimed by my Ex's Dad & His Friend

A Ménage Romance

Claimed by My Ex's Dad & His Friend

A Ménage Romance

Part of the
Eggplant Canyon Series

Sylvie Haas

Claimed by my Ex's Dad & His Friend: A Ménage Romance

Copyright © 2022 by Sylvie Haas

All rights reserved.

No portion of this book may be reproduced in any form without written permission from the publisher or author, except as permitted by U.S. copyright law.

Ebook ISBN: 978-1-950166-80-0

paperback ISBN: 978-1-950166-46-6

Cover Design: Mr. Haas

Contents

Eggplant Canyon Map	VII
Blurb	VIII
1. One Madison	1
2. Two Madison	9
3. Three Jayce	18
4. Four Madison	26
5. Five Elijah	40
6. Six Jayce	46
7. Seven Madison	54

8. Eight 69
   Elijah

9. Nine 73
   Jayce

10. Ten 85
    Madison

11. Eleven 89
    Jayce

12. Epilogue 99
    Elijah

More by Sylvie Haas 108

Sylvie Haas Freebies 109

About the Author 110

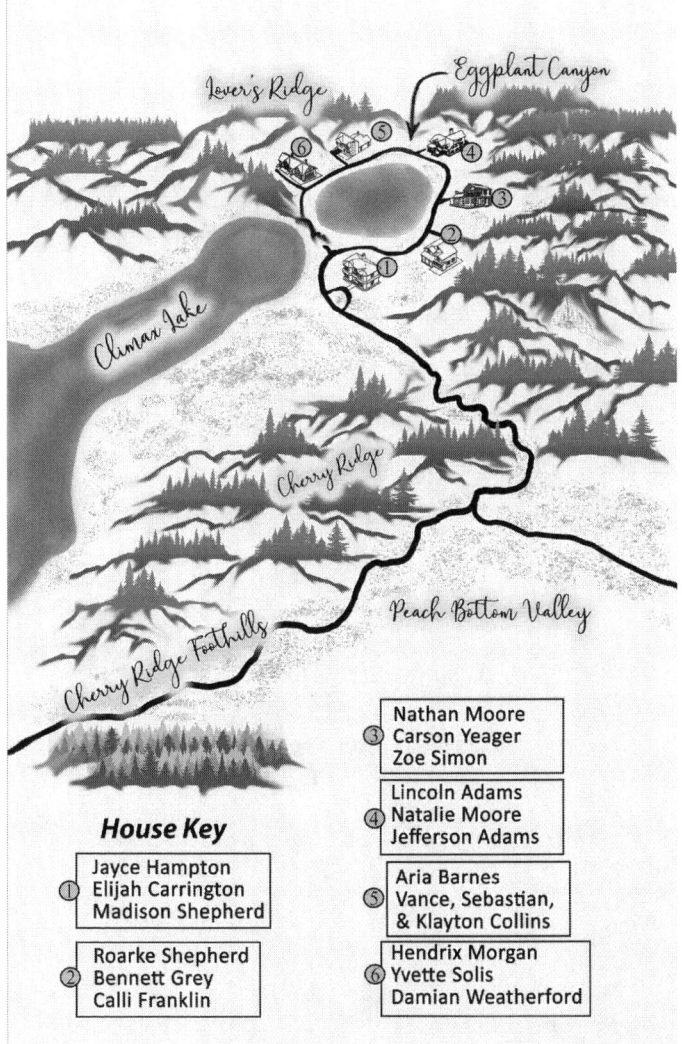

House Key

① Jayce Hampton
  Elijah Carrington
  Madison Shepherd

② Roarke Shepherd
  Bennett Grey
  Calli Franklin

③ Nathan Moore
  Carson Yeager
  Zoe Simon

④ Lincoln Adams
  Natalie Moore
  Jefferson Adams

⑤ Aria Barnes
  Vance, Sebastian,
  & Klayton Collins

⑥ Hendrix Morgan
  Yvette Solis
  Damian Weatherford

Blurb

I thought I wanted the boy next door, until I figured out his dad is one of the real men I crave.

Maybe it's revenge.

Maybe desires can only be repressed for so long.

Maybe my brain is just a scrambled mess since my boyfriend cheated on me. This is the same boyfriend who'd insisted we wait until marriage, much to my dismay.

The only thing that's clear is that I've waited too long to be with a man, and now I want two of them... My ex's dad and his friend, whose name I don't even know.

Does that mean I'm wired wrong? Maybe. But all of my pent-up frustrations beg for release and I'm about to find out if these men will accept me.

My motivation may be questionable, but these men are definitely the answer.

If you love dirty-talking men who have over-the-top ideas of how to please their woman and want to give her babies, these guys are your answer, too!

One

Madison

Crossing the mountain ridge into Eggplant Canyon, I can't believe I'm moving back to my dad's house on the eve of my first job. But when a last-minute position to teach kindergarten was offered, I spent the morning packing my tiny apartment, made the six-hour drive, and now I'm ready to tuck myself into bed.

I want to be well-rested for the mandatory district training day tomorrow.

The house is dark as I make the familiar turn into the driveway. My dad texted to let me know that he got called into the hospital. Nothing new there.

Carrying a couple suitcases with my essentials inside, I don't bother to call my boyfriend, who was my next-door neighbor growing up. I haven't been able to get hold of him for the last few days, but I chalked it up to him being busy with his med school application. The disconnect is symbolic of how well our long-distance relationship has worked out while we attended different universities. Dating was so much easier when we just walked across the grass to see each other.

If he listened to the series of four voice messages I left, he would know that I had a sudden change of plans. It's not that I expected him to drop everything and come back to see me since he's only an hour away, I just wanted to share my excitement.

As I open the curtains in my bedroom to enjoy the moonlight over the mountains, I'm certain he didn't listen.

Otherwise, he would have at least had the decency to close his blinds…I hope.

My phone falls from my hand. I don't bother to pick it up.

My heart breaks as everything I thought I knew about the cute, ambitious, and respectful boy next door, who I've saved my virginity for, bangs some chick.

He was the one to say we shouldn't have sex until we're married. That's not something you just forget. Is it something against me personally? We were supposed to have a future. How long has this been going on?

Dreams shatter far easier than they're built. I can't tear my eyes off the naked tangle of their bodies. How long have I been a fool?

Brett, my suddenly *ex*-boyfriend, hadn't wanted to risk either of our careers with an unplanned pregnancy.

My dad had talked to him about the rigors of med school and how it was really hard to raise a child while going through it. Waiting made sense. Watch out for our futures. A little ridiculous since all I wanted to do was be a mom, but my dad insisted I plan on a career since relationships can go wrong.

Like right now.

My heart splits in two.

The fatigue from my long day channels into anger.

All of my pent-up sexual frustration has been for naught. What's his endgame? I would have fucked him. I'd begged actually. Not a proud moment, but I had. And he'd had the nerve to tell me I should be able to control my urges better.

Fucking hell, I'd thought I was an over-sexed freak for all of my naughty thoughts he refused to entertain. And for the ones he didn't know about, like the ones that involved his dad.

It looks like we both had secrets, but mine didn't hurt anyone.

I force myself to look away. This is over. And I'm going to make sure he doesn't have any wiggle room to sweet talk his way out of it.

I rush downstairs and out of my house, across the grass to his front door, and don't bother knocking.

"Madison?" Brett's father, Jayce, calls out as I storm past his office, which is just off the entry. I don't have to look to know that he's at his desk, he almost always is. Concern has replaced the swoon-worthiness of the wealthy CEO's usual deep voice. I don't care. If he, in any way, taught his son to be a cheater, he's as despicable as his spawn.

As I stride through their living room, I question how I was able to forget his dad could be home. Apparently, I'm drunk on the toxic cocktail of exhaustion, anger, and tunnel vision, and it's served with a blanket of shame. I never forget about his dad—the lingering glances I sometimes catch him sneaking, the tension in his jaw every time I gave Brett a peck on the cheek, or my imaginary belief that he made himself scarce when I was around because he secretly wanted me too—which are all more reasons I thought something was wrong with me.

I would never cheat on my boyfriend. Especially not with his dad.

But if anyone had read my mind... Every time Jayce called me Madison, never the nickname Madi that everyone else used, it made me feel so sexy, so desirable. Not the girl-next-door his son dated, but the woman...never mind. It's my given name, not a seduction. More proof that I'm not wired quite right.

I quicken my pace to get up the stairs when I hear Jayce behind me.

"Wait...I thought you two broke up." So he does know what Brett's doing.

"We are now." My blanket of shame is starting to suffocate me. It's hard enough to find out my boyfriend is a loser, much less reveal it in front of my secret crush. But my freight train of anger is in motion.

Throwing Brett's bedroom door open, I want to vomit. Seeing him with another woman from my window was one thing, but up close...it's far too real. What had I planned on doing? Pieces of thoughts form a maelstrom of hurt and chaos in my mind.

Brett and his fuck buddy realize I'm in the room. They break their kiss to look at me. The other part of them stays together. Gag. I need a plan, and fast. I've done, or not done, everything Brett asked. Look where that got me. I won't be the victim.

Think. Think. Think.

"Madi?" Brett lifts up. My urge to vomit heightens.

The thinking train derails. I rush forward, shrugging my blanket of shame. I'm not the one at fault. There are a million things I want to say to him but words fail me as I rear my fist back.

When I thrust it forward, a primal scream erupts from me, sparing me from having to hear his nose break. Wow! That felt good. Like I'm doing all women a favor by standing up for myself.

Brett falls onto the girl, making a horrible sound as he grips his face and rolls off. Thankfully the sheet spares me the details that are no longer my business.

He doesn't deserve a chance to explain.

Before anyone can say anything coherent, I spin around and rush out of the room as quickly as I entered, not bothering to close the door.

Turning the corner, tears blur my vision. I plow into Jayce. His hard body becomes a wall supporting me. His hands circle my waist and for way longer than a split second, I hope Brett comes out of his room and catches his father holding me.

Maybe there is something wrong with me. I'm not usually the type of person to want revenge.

I shift my eyes to the stairwell past Jayce. "Umm, sorry, I need to go."

His grip tightens.

"I've got you." His tone has never been so low and possessive. "Let's go downstairs."

"I'm fine." I try to move but not enough to convince him that's what I want. I give in to his grip, his protection. My sex tingles. My entire body tingles. And when he pulls me into his chest, his arms firm around my back, and if I can believe myself, his lips in my hair, and something very hard against my belly. For the first time ever, I question that being wired wrong might not be such a bad thing.

"You deserve to be treated better than that." His words. His tone. His belief in me. They're turning me to mush. They're giving me hope for something I know better than to believe in.

"A *real man* would treat me better." It's supposed to be a jab at his son, his *child*, but as I angle my head up and get lost in Jayce's possessive gaze, I can't be sure of my intent. My momentary bravado lures me into the forbidden.

The sincerity in his gaze penetrates me. It's how a man should look at a woman he loves. Not that I've experienced it until this moment. But it's clear. It has me questioning everything.

It's too much. I'm hurt. I'm mad. I'm making things up.

Before I embarrass myself, I pull away from his comfort and warmth. I drift my hands down both handrails, and stride to the front door. The cold metal of the handle is my ticket to freedom, but movement in Jayce's office catches my attention.

Shit. Is someone else here? I have the door in motion as I turn my face to see.

The handsome stranger is chiseled in all of the right ways. Enough to make me misstep. To crack the door into the side of my head.

"Oomph." I stumble back, unsure if I've lost balance from the collision or if the ravenous look in his eyes, which I certainly made up, made my legs go weak.

He circles the desk. The look intensifies. I can't let him touch me. I still can't breathe from Jayce's contact. Why am I thinking he would do that? I must have hit my head harder than I thought.

Steadying myself, I run out of the Hampton household as fast as possible.

That should be it. Brett and I are done. I'm not going to pretend that Mister Hampton or his friend lust after me. I'm going to give myself a minute for an impromptu pity party then do my best to get some sleep before the school district's training day for new hires.

But this night can't go wrong enough.

When I get home, my curtains are still open. My house still faces the Hampton's house, because despite it feeling like the entire world shifted on its axis and everything tilted out of whack, nothing has changed.

I'm still wildly turned on by Brett's dad. And his friend. It's not just in the lingering sensation of his fingers wrapped around my waist like he didn't want to let go, or the incredible hardness of his body as he held me tightly. Or the way both of them looked at me like I was theirs.

I'm standing at my floor-to-ceiling window, my hands gripped on the curtains on either side ready to pull them closed, and once again, I can't move.

Jayce's silhouette is in his window, one that I know to be their entertainment room. He's backlit by a lamp. His hands are braced just above shoulder height on either side of the window. If I can trust my eyes, he's staring at me.

Or more accurately, he's staring at my window, because up until a split second ago, I wasn't in it.

But now that I am, he's not moving, so I guess that makes my first assumption correct...he's staring at me.

I like it.

And when his friend walks up behind him, I like it even more.

Two

Madison

My dad and I were hanging out but he had somewhere to go. I suppose that was his way of avoiding saying he had something to do at the hospital. Why bother hiding it?

It's fine. I'm exhausted, so I retreat to my bedroom.

For the last three days, I've been swamped with district training and revamping my lesson plans.

It's been a wild, exhausting ride. The training alone would have been enough since I had to switch gears from first grade to kindergarten to take this position, which meant revamping my lesson plans. But I'd also taken on the after-school program, which meant extra long days and an entire other lesson plan.

All of the hecticness aside, I'm glad I made a last-minute change to accept the teaching position close to where I grew up. Once I settle into a routine, I ought to be able to see old friends. Or am I putting it off because I'm a chicken?

My former best friend, Calli, is here and I really want to make amends. I need to apologize for dismissing her concerns years before and being a pretty horrific best friend.

What if her number changed? I'll just think she's ghosting me. Which I would deserve. Plus, I must have left my phone downstairs. I'll text her tomorrow. *Bawk*

Slipping my silky robe over my pajama set, a tank top and short shorts, I stare at my closed curtains. I could easily say that I've been too busy to bother opening them...for three days.

The truth is that I'm worried what I'll see if I do. *Bawk. Bawk.*

It's not Brett's window that worries me anymore. He left town the day after someone broke his nose. Word travels fast in a small town, but thankfully the detail about me is missing.

Each night when I've crawled into bed, I've stared at the curtains, pretending that if I open them Jayce will still be in his window, hands braced on the edges, waiting on me. Wanting to make sure I'm okay. Desperate to show me how a man should treat a woman.

This is when his friend usually enters the fantasy, and I let both men tend to the needs I've been denied.

I've gone off the deep end.

I thought it was a twisted rebound fantasy...wanting my ex's dad and his friend. The truth is that I've always wanted Jayce. I kept trying to force the desire into an inaccessible part of my brain since I was dating his son.

Now that I'm single, I'd hoped to get Jayce and his friend out of my system by letting my fantasies run wild while I pleasured myself.

That took things the wrong direction. Thoughts of them morphed into what I can only describe as an obsession. It's clouding my ability to think, even when I'm at work.

And that's too much. I can't lose this job.

I moved back home not only because my tough-love dad developed a soft spot and let me stay for free, but I want to work on our relationship. I'd felt alone when I was away at school. Now that I'm an adult with a job, I think he'll be able to relate to me more—thus the added reason not to lose it. While I was growing up, he'd been so busy with patients and creating new programs at the hospital that I hardly knew him.

Which is why when he got a text and said he needed to leave tonight, I wasn't surprised.

I laugh out loud. Considering how many hours of the day I'm putting into my job, the apple didn't fall far from the tree. At least we spend time together each evening since he agreed he could do better.

It's weird recognizing that my dad's obsession with work is rooted in wanting to bring better healthcare to our little neck of the woods. Too bad it came with the sacrifice of not being around much when I was little. Not so different than my love of kids and wanting to give them the best start possible.

My thoughts deviate back to Jayce. This can't be healthy. Perhaps Brett was right, my interest in sex is—No. No more of that thinking. He lied to me. He cheated on me. He made me feel dirty for wanting sex.

But wanting sex with his dad…that has to qualify as dirty.

Perhaps if I open my curtains, I'll find out just how dirty he is.

I rub my hands over my face. No. I'll pull the curtains back so I can accept that he doesn't brood in his window each night. My fantasy is clearly out of control. I need to find someone else to fantasize about.

I tamp down the idea of his friend. Too awkward. Too old. Actually, the friend is younger. And I'm back down one of my lust spirals.

Pushing both panels back a few inches, my breath hitches when the light is on in the Hampton's game room.

Curling my fingers around the edges of my curtains, I tuck the fabric to my chest. The flutters and tingles rushing through me are wrong.

I force my gaze to Brett's window. Nothing. No light. No Brett. No feelings. Yay? Shouldn't I feel something?

Movement pulls my attention back to the illuminated window. Jayce enters the room.

My skin tickles every time he looks my way. I'm sure it's all in my head. With my lights off, he can't see me anyway.

Angling one thigh into the other, I shift my hips to ease the mounting tension. I'll have to throw myself back into the dating scene. Find a guy who doesn't criticize me for wanting to have sex. Should I list on my profile that I'm looking for real men? I snicker at my misstep...looking for a real *man*. Maybe someone older?

My heartbeat quickens as I consider what it would be like to have more than one. Is that a deviant thought? Maybe if Brett hadn't deprived me, I wouldn't be so wound up.

Drawing the curtains to have a couple feet of opening, I sit on the plush chaise that faces the window from only a few feet away. Growing up, I used it for relaxing and reading, staring out at the mountains, and yes, staring at Brett. He never did the same. And when he caught me in my window one night, he texted to tell me it wasn't polite to watch people through their windows.

It was one of many desires I had that he didn't share. He'd made me feel naughty for the things I wanted.

But with my lights off, no one in their house can see into my room. I know from leaving my stuffed animals on the chaise then trying to see them from Brett's window. He may not have wanted to watch, but that didn't stop me. So many nights I'd willed my dirty thoughts would go away. So many nights they didn't.

So many nights I watched his dad instead. Nothing sexy, except for the way he makes walking through a room look hot, but those are my little secrets.

I settle in at the perfect angle where I can see Jayce, and get comfortable enough to take care of myself. I swear he keeps looking at my window. Can he see me?

Nearly breathless, I monitor his glances. Four more pauses on my window give no indication he can see in. But he's looking. I like that.

Swallowing hard, I slide my hand into the waistband of my shorts. My fingers brush over my curls. This is probably illegal. I'll blame it on emotional scarring from Brett denying me sex while he was boning someone else.

Lazily dragging my finger through my juices, I let out a sigh. I'm so wet it's ridiculous. Not sure my thing for older guys would translate well into real-life dating, but it's good fantasy fodder.

You deserve to be treated better than that. Jayce's words carry so loudly through my mind that I look around my room. Not here. He's still safely two panes of glass and lawns away.

I relax into the seat. Jayce moves back and forth across the room, around the pool table, occasionally stepping out of sight, but never for long.

Succumbing to my imagination, I pretend I'm on the pool table. He's circling me. Studying me the way I've watched him study the angle for a pool shot.

Jayce's gaze lands on my window, a little longer this time. My breath catches in my throat. I don't breathe again until he looks away. If he could see, there's no way he would have looked away. Right?

A hint of guilt niggles in my mind...unless he wishes his son's ex-girlfriend would get control of herself, and quit being a slutty little voyeur. Or is it a naughty exhibitionist? Is it possible to be both? It seems wrong that I think of myself as naughty and slutty, but that turns me on too.

He studies the table, rakes a hand through his hair, and leans over. I double-down circling my clit. How good would his tongue feel?

I moan and sink my fingers inside of me. Forget his tongue. What would his cock feel like? Instead of telling me he wants to wait until we're married, he'd show me how a real man pleases a woman.

Hand, tongue, cock...so many orgasms...I stir myself into a frenzy. Another moan escapes my lips, my eyes fall shut, and I drop my head back as I draw myself closer.

Light streams into my consciousness. Is it the start of my orgasm? I'm so close. It's not my orgasm though. What's happening?

I blink hard against the brightness coming from the hallway as I take in my dad's voice, "Madi, you okay?"

He was supposed to leave already.

I scramble to pull my robe over myself, get my hand out of my shorts, and rectify my spread-eagle position.

"I'm fine," I blurt. Please don't let him realize what I'm doing. He can't see Jayce's window from where my door is. Tempering my voice with annoyance, I shift so I'm facing over the back of the chaise and continue, "I was looking at the stars, relaxing."

Feigning a glance outside, my sights catch on Jayce standing squarely in his window. This can't be happening.

"Hmm, didn't know you liked to do that." My dad steps into my room, extending his hand and my phone. "You left this downstairs."

No. No. No. I can't let him come over.

"Set it on my dresser." I point to the other side of the door. "Thanks, Dad. Catch you in the morning."

He follows my cue—problem one solved.

"You know. It's nice having you home and getting to spend quality time with you. I love you, Madi."

"Love you too, Dad." I don't have time for a trip down memory lane or correcting him that I don't want to use that nickname anymore. And I don't dare look out the window.

"You worked hard this week. You deserve some R and R. I'm proud of you."

Maybe not if you knew what you just interrupted. My stomach is in knots waiting as he steps out and closes the door. Darkness cloaks my room once again.

A second passes before I turn to the window. Nothing could prepare me for what I see. Jayce is waiting for me. Exactly the way I imagined in my fantasies—his hands braced on either side of the window.

I draw a slow breath. He must have seen me. He can't see me now. What do I do?

Do I want to find out how a real man treats a woman?

Three

Jayce

I need to get my head straight, which is clearly not happening since I'm jacking off to the remnant of another dream about Madison before I roll myself into the shower. That's four times in the eight hours since she broke me.

She knew Brett wasn't home. The only light in the house was for the room I was in. The room I can best see her bedroom window from. No matter how I try to spin what I saw, she was masturbating while watching me.

My balls tighten and my cock reminds me that my hand is a sorry substitute for the only thing I've wanted the last few years.

Does my son's ex-girlfriend have a thing for me too? I'm way too old. Besides, I've always been married to my job, which is why my wife left long ago. I have to give her credit though, she stuck with me until I made enough she could walk away and be financially sound. Brett used to go back and forth between our houses when she lived over the hill, but when she got remarried and moved across the country, he stayed with me, even though we didn't get along great.

I assumed Madison was his reason for staying, but finding out he was cheating on her makes that questionable. Why didn't he break up with her like he told me he had? Why treat someone like that? Especially someone so...Madison.

She's smart, beautiful, and has a wicked innocence. And as of Monday night, I can add having an excellent right hook to her list of attributes. Didn't see that one coming, not that she's timid, she has a fiery side, but it's always been tempered by how sweet and kind she is.

Now that she's single, I want her more than ever.

Gripping my cock, stroking faster, I recall her minty scent, so subtle I'd only caught hints of it before. Never let myself get close enough. But three nights ago, for a few precious seconds, I held her in my hands and pulled her body into mine, unable to stop myself from protecting her.

That's when my delusions started. I would have bet my life that her expression shifted from hurt and anger at my son to the desire to be protected and cared for. I'd even convinced myself that she wanted it from me.

As my mind drifts back to last night, her head dropped back, neck exposed, hand in her pants, I blow my load into the sheets.

The maid is coming today, but this is too much to leave for her. I'll throw these in the washer. Won't I appear helpful.

Moving through another day, questioning my ability to ensure my company remains maximally profitable, the question remains… If Madison wasn't thinking of me, why did she have her curtains open?

I make it through another day only because the clock never stops. I've wasted most of it sitting in my office wondering how the hell I can explain to Madison how badly I need her. I can't even explain it to myself.

Elijah, the CEO I'm working on a merger with is supposed to come over to my house tonight. He'd been at my house the night all hell broke loose. Reasonably, it made him uncomfortable, so he'd left early, leaving me to sort shit out with my son.

Luckily, we're good for tonight. We've been meeting a minimum of every Friday night for a few weeks, on the verge of clenching a huge deal. But my craving to see Madison again clouds my judgment. I pull up his number on my phone, ready to cancel.

My secretary pops her head into my office. "Have a nice weekend, Mister Hampton."

Pulling my finger away from Elijah's phone number, I check the clock. "Time to go already?"

"Some of us actually have lives outside of work. You should try it some time." Her playful comment, one she's egged me on about before, hits hard today.

"You might be on to something." I let her words sink in for a few minutes after she leaves. Elijah would be pissed if I bail since our schedules are full. I'll keep the meeting with him, but I need to work on getting a personal life. One where I do more than work and jack off to my son's ex-girlfriend.

But apparently, that will start tomorrow because I work a few more hours then, when I get home, I head straight to the game room where I can keep an eye on Madison's window. I'll close the curtains when Elijah arrives.

Headlights from a car pull out from her house but a quick assessment tells me it's her dad. Roarke already hates me. He'd kill me if he knew I wanted to fuck his daughter. What he wouldn't understand is that I want to do so much more. Protect her from jerks like my son.

We've been at odds for a few years now, never seeing eye to eye on anything, but he took it to an all new level by cheating on Madison.

Elijah messaged that he was going to be later than normal, so it's already dark. I'm already hopeful. My balls are already blue.

I'm rubbing chalk over the tip of my cue when light causes me to do a double take. Madison's window. The curtains are wide open. This time a soft light illuminates her as she stands in the opening. It's purposeful. Her body is angled to the side, she's clutching the front of her robe, and I can't tell what she's looking at. Something in the room. Why am I not her first thought? Why am I jealous?

Dragging her fingers through her hair, she twirls the dark strands.

The pool chalk clatters somewhere under the table.

She's playing with me. She wants me to see. Fuck. My dick is hard. How is my son such an idiot?

Please don't let this be another dream. It's so real. I need it to be real. I've filled her with my seed so many times, only to wake up with my dick in my hand. That can't keep happening.

Our eyes catch for the briefest of seconds, but for that tiny slip of time, I'm electrified. She knows I can see her.

I lean against the end of the pool table closest to the window. What's under her baby blue robe today? Nothing? A guy can hope.

She mills back and forth past the window frame as seconds tick away. My cock gets harder with each one. The seductress is playing innocent. I'm reassured that with the way our houses face, none of our neighbors can see in our windows.

I'm dying to strip bare and relieve my cock of the agony it's facing trapped in my jeans. I brazenly rub a hand over it. Can't take them off just yet, but fuck I want to. I have half a mind to head over to her house so I can sink my dick into her tight pussy and give her as many orgasms as she can handle.

Has my son even bothered to make her come? That shouldn't be my concern, but as soon as I knew he didn't treat her right, I wanted to know the extent. I'd hate it if any man had wronged her. I'd hate it if any man treated her well. The only thing I can handle is her being mine.

Fuck. The craving I've had for her for far too long is out of control.

She pauses in the window, looking into the distance. I'm fairly certain her busyness is all part of the show. My fiery little angel wants me to see, but isn't sure how far to take it.

She's not mine.

That's why I should get a grip. Look away. Close the blinds. It's a show. She wants to hurt Brett. There can't be any more to it than that. Then I remember the look in her eyes and the way her body willingly sank into mine for that stolen moment, and I'm not so sure.

She eases her fingers down the center of her robe, draping it open around her bra.

My cock twitches.

Holy babymaker. The small strip of fabric that dips between her legs is barely enough to be called panties. I could slip my cock around those in a heartbeat.

I squeeze my cock through my jeans. My free hand clutches the edge of the pool table, anchoring me. I can't go to her. The things I want to do to her aren't right. Even if she'd have me, I can't be her rebound...or revenge...I want to be her reason.

"Hey honey, I'm home," Elijah calls from way too close. How did I not hear him come in?

Damn it. I lean forward to lower the blinds to protect Madison, to keep her as my own.

"Fuck." Elijah's seen her.

Disappointment sinks through me that I didn't act fast enough. I let her down. Elijah is grabbing my arm, pulling it away from the blinds. I'm about to shove him away when I realize she isn't hiding.

Madison toys with the edge of her bra as she watches us. Does she want him to see?

No other words are exchanged. I struggle to make sense of what's happening. She could walk away. Choices are being made. Very erotic choices. And it's getting harder to deny them.

Then she turns away and reality slaps me upside the head. She was frozen in panic. I can't be a part of hurting her. This has to end. I reach for the blinds.

Her robe slinks down her body, pooling on the floor.

What the fuck? My jaw hits the floor with it.

Her thong leaves little to the imagination. She's utter perfection. The curve from her waist to her hips looks even better than it felt. I can't decide if I'm glad she's including Elijah or not. Does that mean she's just having fun, teasing her ex's dad and his friend?

I'll spank that pretty little ass of hers if that's the case. And in a thong like that, she'll feel every bit of the sting.

My entire body tenses when she turns around. She's rubbing a hand over her bra. For us. Dropping a hand between her legs. For us. Do I care if this is all just a game to her? Can I play nice? There's very little chance of that.

"We should stop. This is wrong on so many levels." But my actions speak louder than words.

"How old is she?" Elijah's voice is strained.

"Old enough."

Four

Madison

I stare at my ceiling after sleeping in. Nowhere pressing to be this morning.

My brain replays last night as it did numerous ways in my dreams. Maybe there is something wrong with me. It's not just that I gave Jayce a window show or that I didn't stop when his friend arrived. I want to do it again. They enjoyed me in ways Brett never allowed.

And now that I'd whet my whistle, I crave more. I'd played it safe, closing the curtains after rubbing my hands over my body.

This sexual awakening, or whatever it is, empowers me. I'm more alive, more grounded, more connected to *them* than I've ever been to anyone.

I just don't understand why.

Ugh, I roll onto my side. Who the hell am I kidding?

Where do I see this going? It's not like we're building a relationship. Except that damn connection part that I can't shake. Is this how people feel when they're intimate with each other? Did Brett leave me hanging too long and now I'm dry humping any guy who comes along?

Okay, that's an overreaction. There are exactly two guys I'd like to dry hump. And that's another problem. I'd be happy to do away with the dry part of that. I'm anything but.

Fresh air might do me good. I head onto the second-story deck, where I can't see his house. I want to shout to the mountains that I'm in love, or at least lust. That's better kept to myself though. Plus, it doesn't matter since what we're doing isn't exactly a deep, emotional relationship built on loads of common interests and intertwined futures.

They're just enjoying a free peep show. I roll my eyes at myself. Am I playing with fire? I shudder at how badly I want to get burned.

I work up the nerve to text Calli. If I'm going to make amends, I'll have to be persistent.

I'm thrilled when she replies.

Calli: *Yeah, we need to talk*

So maybe she's still mad, but ready to reconcile if I am. She has a break, which is only an hour from now. She works a ton of hours at the diner, but I haven't set foot in there since getting home. Brett used to take me there a lot. Too much. Guess it kept us from being anywhere private. So many things with him make sense now. So many still don't.

"Madi," my dad barks as I open the door to come back inside.

"Just a second." I detour downstairs to the kitchen to see what he wants, then I need to get showered and ready to meet Calli.

I stop in my tracks when my dad waves his phone at me. He's fuming. My stomach drops. I've only done one bad thing.

"What the hell were you thinking? Are you trying to get fired?"

I break out in a cold sweat. How do I start my explanation?

Must have been rhetorical questions because he continues. "I may not have been a good, doting father, but fuck, I raised you better than to run around punching people in the face."

My brain does a classic record scratch as I move the needle to replay his statement. He's talking about Brett? Okay, I've done two bad things, but punching Brett was for the right reasons. And I'd conveniently not mentioned it to my dad since he thinks Brett is perfect.

He points to the barstools. "Sit down."

I comply, taking the stool at the end closest to me while he sits at the other end. His elbows rest on the marble counter and he rubs his temples.

"You're really lucky Brett understands the importance of discretion. He could have filed a police report. This could have been a disaster."

My dad's taking his side? How did he even find out? He works at the hospital but was supposedly out with a friend that night. That's on him if he lied to me so he could sneak to work. Anyway, why isn't he asking me why I hit Brett?

"I'm not lucky. I'm...heartbroken." The word whooshes from my lips. Emotion tears through me. My shoulders slump. I need a hug. I need to know that Brett wasn't cheating on me the whole time. I need my dad to trust me.

"Dad, he was...he..."

The word won't come out. Am I ashamed? It's not my fault Brett cheated. I did, or rather didn't do, everything he asked.

Dad straightens up and rests his hand on the next stool. "He told me you two broke up."

The lack of compassion in my father's tone reminds me of how unavailable he's always been, not just physically, during my childhood. It's not worth explaining. He won't even care.

"Yeah."

"That's not a reason to punch someone, Madi. But I had your friend Aria, you know she's working at the hospital, right? Anyway, I had her pull the file. She confirmed that Brett said he tripped."

"How do you know Aria's my friend?" As if that's my biggest problem. I'm just shocked that he might have paid attention at some point.

He shrugs. "She mentioned it one day."

The glimmer of hope that he paid attention to any part of my life is squashed.

"You're missing the point, Madi. This is a small town. If we tarnish our reputations, we'll be judged, especially someone like you who's just starting out. If the school found out, they might worry you'll punch a student."

"I would never punch a student." Frustration turns to anger. Again. Is that what being home is going to be like? All I can think about is getting back to my window. Releasing my pent-up energy with men who understand me. But do they? What do I really know about them?

A huff pounds through my chest. My own dad doesn't get me. My boyfriend, ex-boyfriend, didn't get me. Jayce and his friend on the other hand... They let me be me. They help me feel normal.

My dad walks over and sets a hand on my shoulder.

"I know, Madi. You're a kind, tender soul. Honestly, I questioned Brett's accusation."

"Really?" Are we having a bonding moment? Maybe Dad's not a total jerk.

"Yeah, that's why I had Aria pull his medical chart. There was a note in it that said the doctor had questioned Brett's explanation, but he stuck to his story. He protected you."

Not exactly bonding after all.

He squeezes my shoulder. "Don't worry. You're secret's safe with me. And I've got Brett under control too. I came through on the letter of recommendation for med school for him, so he won't be telling anyone you assaulted him."

"Assault? And you did what?" I shrug from my dad's grasp, stumble as my foot catches on the bar stool leg, and manage to catch myself before falling.

"I know it's hard to hear that I wrote a letter of recommendation for your former boyfriend, but he's a good guy. He's always had an impressive way of going after what he wants. Medical school requires a lot of hard work, no time for relationships, I should know. Give it a little time and you'll be ready to move on. You'll find a nice boy."

A nice *boy*? What the hell? I'm regretting moving home more and more with each word out of his mouth. But if I hadn't moved back home, I'd still be pining away for the wrong Mister Hampton.

"You're right. I'll find someone perfect for me, because it definitely wasn't Brett. And it most certainly won't be a *boy*." I snap the last word and leave him fumbling to clarify he didn't mean boy.

I tune him out well before I get to my room and slam the door. The closed curtains beckon. I rush to them, placing my hands on the center hems, pausing for a moment. Am I doing this for the right reasons? All I've ever wanted is to be seen.

Throwing the curtains back, my soul flickers to life. Jayce is sitting on his deck. His head snaps my direction, and the flicker rages to an inferno.

My phone dings from where I dropped it on my dresser, reminding me that I barely have time to get showered and out the door to meet Calli. I can't miss this perfect opportunity with Jayce though.

Glancing around, I confirm the world has boiled down to Jayce and me. I'm a touch sad his friend isn't around, but after this, I bet his friend will be back.

Teasing him in the light of day is a little intimidating. A lot intriguing. Turning away from the window, I remove my pajama shirt. I wrap my arm over my bare chest as I walk through my room, picking the clothes I plan to wear, and laying them on my bed.

Assuming he's still watching, because...why not...I wave over my shoulder as I head to my bathroom. The privacy of the smaller room gives me a chance to think. This might not amount to anything more than some fun, but I'll only know if I try.

I adjust the water temperature while I sort my emotions. They're so intense, I can't peel them apart. Excitement, pride, fear, anger. There's a little bit of everything. I'm way out of my comfort zone. But my dad's right. People don't get what they want by waiting for it to come to them.

Which gives me another idea. Have all the fun I can. I unlock the bathroom window and slide it open, pretending not to notice Jayce. All he can see through this window is from my waist up. My breasts are on full display. I bend down, stripping my shorts, lift them high enough he can see, then set them on the window sill before stepping into the shower.

I wash up quickly so he doesn't lose interest and I give him another peep of my perky tits while I dry off. Then I cross in front of my bedroom window in only a towel. Out of sight, I slip my panties on but forgo my bra. Clutching my sundress against my chest, I position myself in front of the window again.

The glance I allowed myself reveals that he slipped his sunglasses on and kicked back in his chair. Nice job disguising what he's looking at. We can both pretend to be disinterested.

With my back to him, I slip my arms into the dress, angle it overhead, and let it slink down my body, shifting my hips to help it. I've never experienced a rush like this. I'm about to explode with that thing I still don't understand.

I don't look over my shoulder as I grab my purse and head out of my bedroom. It's not until I'm in the driveway that I look up at his deck. He's standing. Watching me. Another spear of excitement pierces me. Am I an exhibitionist?

I glance to see if anyone's nearby. The mayor, who lives across our little lake is looking my direction. I feel caught before I even do anything. He's not looking at me though. His gaze is next door. Peeking over, I see our neighbors, Nathan and Carson, are rather cozy with a girl I went to high school with. Interesting. Stealing a second glance, I confirm that she's sandwiched between them. Okay, if she can have two guys, so can I. I'm going for it.

Wiggling my fingers in a wave, I turn back to Jayce. "Gotta go meet someone. I hope your friend is back tonight."

I pull my car door open, jump inside, and force myself not to look again. There's something in the unknown, not giving him a chance to take control that's totally getting me off. I have to calm myself before I can start the car.

Too many years were wasted on a single *boy*. *Men* are what I need. But first I have to win my best friend back.

A short trip down memory lane while I drive into town revisits the conversation that drove us apart. She'd warned me that Brett was using me. I'd thought I had the best comeback when I pointed out he couldn't be because we weren't having sex.

It devolved from there when I called her jealous and didn't need anyone telling me who I should or shouldn't date, then she got mad and went out with friends we didn't know and got arrested, and I didn't bail her out. She's not from the expensive neighborhood I live in, and that was the only time money ever became an issue between us. Yeah, it was rough, but I'm ready to admit that she was right about Brett not being in love with me, although I still don't understand why he didn't just dump me.

Callie's in the corner booth when I arrive. Our old favorite awaits—an order of cheese fries. I didn't think to bring a peace offering. Trusting her with my secret will have to do. We never talked about older guys. I have no idea what she'll think. But no need to worry about that until we reconnect.

She jumps up and gives me a hug. I almost cry. I hold her tight. Friendship is such a precious commodity. "I'm so sorry I was the worst best friend ever."

"Is that why you're so hard to replace? Let's let all of that stay in the past."

Her tone carries more remorse than I expect. We agree that we were teens making bad choices. Time to embrace our hard-earned maturity.

We each take a side of the booth. "Yeah, I've been without a bestie since I left for college." I pick up a cheese fry and point it toward her. "Gossip on the lips. Cheese fries on the hips."

She busts out laughing, grabs a fry, and taps it to mine the way we used to. "My metabolism isn't as forgiving as it was in high school, even with running around the diner all day, but yes. I'd like to try this best friend thing again, which is why we need to talk."

A strangle sound, like really fast nonsense talking starts and she grabs her phone.

"Is that a Minion ringtone?"

Whatever the text message says, it made her nervous. She shoves the phone back on the table, face down. "Yeah."

"What happened to *Bad to the Bone*?"

"I relate better to crazy purple Minions now."

"Well, I did a bad to the bone thing."

"Really?"

"I should have listened to you about Brett. I'm sure you heard we broke up…" I'm 'chomping at the bit' level of excited to tell her the rest of the story.

She nods and grimaces. "Yep, and Aria happened to come into the diner the day after Brett's accident." She puts air quotes on the word. "Aria might need to revisit her medical privacy rules because she said they think someone hit him. Based on that grin you're wearing, I'm going to ask something really crazy. Was it you?"

My grin grows and I nod.

"Wow, I'm sorry he made you that mad. I didn't know you had it in you."

"I didn't either until I caught him screwing someone else."

Calli's mouth falls open. "But…he didn't want to…seriously?"

"I don't get it. But I'm really lucky Brett was so discreet at the hospital." My voice drips with false sincerity.

Calli laughs. "He's not about to admit he got punched by a girl."

"It's okay, just this morning my dad wrote a letter of recommendation for Brett so he'll continue to keep quiet. But Brett only thinks he won. My dad's so career oriented he's blind to why I would do something like that. It would do him good to relax a little. Get laid." My joke falls flat.

Calli looks nervous. "That has to sting." She seems to shrink. "You know I love you, right."

I cup my hand over hers. "It's all good. Not like I'm used to being my dad's priority or anything. I don't know what he does with all of his time. It really can't be healthy to work as much as he does."

"He comes in here once in a while with friends. He's not all work. I don't think he's a bad person, just doesn't know how to be a good dad."

I shrug. "You were right about Brett. You're probably right about my dad too. Moving back home was supposed to be a chance where my dad could see me as an adult and we could try again, but other than free rent, he doesn't offer a lot."

"Will it be hard seeing Brett when he comes back home? Since you're right next door?"

"That's where things get tricky."

"How so?"

Time to bask in my discomfort. But also to make this real. Everything's more real when I share it with Calli. "Have you considered dating an older guy?"

The color drains from her face. "What?"

"It's crazy right, but think about it. They have their shit together. They have a steady job..."

She holds her hand up. "What does this have to do with me?"

"Don't be so nervous, silly. I'm not saying you should date an older guy... I want to. Jayce and I have a thing. And to make it even better. His friend is in on it."

"Jayce, as in Brett's dad?"

I nod. "Date might be a stretch, but I think there's something between us."

"Hold on... His friend? What do you know about him?"

"Not even his name." My exhilaration is quickly tamped down by Calli's lack thereof.

"Seriously, Madi?"

"I switched to Madison."

"Okay, Madison. You barely broke up with Brett a week ago. Are you sure it's not revenge?"

I thought she'd be cooler about this. "I've considered that a million times. It's more. It's like I'm figuring out what I really want in a man. The older guy thing works for me."

"Sorry, it's not the older guy thing. It's just that you were with Brett for so long, you should give yourself some time."

"Right, but you wanted to talk about something, and I went down this giant rabbit hole."

"Don't worry, it was nothing."

"Your face doesn't say it was nothing." My secret reveal went over like a lead balloon. And now she doesn't want to share. I'll have to work a lot harder at being a good friend.

"Calli, we're getting busy," her boss calls.

She waves acknowledgment and says to me, "It can wait. Looks like my break's almost over anyway."

Hanging out with Calli, even for her short break, I'm reminded how much I miss her. But she's wrong about my intentions. I think. She wasn't wrong about Brett. Am I making another mistake?

It doesn't feel wrong. And if it is, I'll get out. Have some fun, and get out.

And if I have it in me to make this more than a window fling, I can lose my virginity to real men.

Five

Elijah

"I hope your friend is back tonight?" I repeat Jayce's explanation of Madison's words. Less than a week ago, she was his son's girlfriend, which makes her motivation highly questionable. That's what the logical part of my brain tells me. Every other fiber of my being tells me this is something more. That the desire I saw in her expression a split second before she cracked the door into her face was real.

I need to accept it for what it is—every guy's fantasy.

"That's what she said." Jayce's voice carries intense disbelief. He's having as much trouble accepting it as I am.

I rake a hand through my hair after knocking another ball into a pocket. Instead of taking another shot, I turn to Jayce. "I don't know if I'm more shocked that she would say that, or that you'd actually call me after she showed her titties off to you. Could have kept her all to yourself." It's hard for me to soak it all in. I haven't told Jayce the extent of my attraction so I'm playing it off as physical for now. But this is big. The physical part is beyond perfect, but it's her boldness to do this of her own free will, and to do it for both of us that makes my entire body ache. Blue balls could take over my existence.

"It's what she wants. And you're here, so it looks like we're all in agreement."

"We can't let this get in the way of our merger."

"Not a chance." Jayce is back to his definitive self.

"You're sure she and your son are done? It wasn't just an argument they're going to patch up? You know this won't play out well if Brett ever finds out."

"They're done, and I'm sure as fuck not going to tell him." The determination in Jayce's voice makes me question if he plans on making sure they stay broken up.

"And if she tells him? We have to consider this could simply be revenge."

Her light flips on and our conversation stops. Her curtains are wide open. Her robe flutters around her as she passes in front of the window.

Jayce points. "This is what she did earlier. Acted like she didn't know I was watching."

She pauses in front of the window, brushing her hair. I'm about to question how consensual this is when she looks at us and smiles. There's no doubt she's consenting. Blood rushes to my cock.

Then she's back to brushing her hair for a few seconds before stepping to where we can't see her.

"My son cheated on her. She's too good for him. I'll never let them get back to—"

She's back without her brush or robe.

"What's wrong with your son?"

"I guess sexy and confident wasn't his type."

Did she turn music on? She's swaying, dancing with herself if I had to guess. Damn shame. We're both rubbing our hands against our straining erections.

I haven't gotten a boner in front of another guy in decades. But there's something between us that keeps this from being awkward. So why do I want to tell him to get his cock out and stroke it?

I shift my gaze back to Madison. I want a piece of her. I want to experience the beautiful side of a woman that will punch a guy in the face while he's fucking another woman. Everything I know about Madison captivates me. Jayce filled me in on her being an honor student, lots of volunteer activities, and so few public displays of affection with Brett.

I have so much catching up to do. I'm jealous that Jayce has known her longer. "You suppose she's shy in public, but in private, she's...like this?"

"If I got my hands on her, she'd have to learn to be loved all the time, not just in private."

Loved. Yeah, I feel the same. It's a lot to process. "You don't think we're taking advantage of her, do you?"

"We're not forcing her into anything."

"Heartbreak can be a bitch. Make you crazy." If there's any reason we shouldn't be playing to the whims of this young woman, I want to address it.

"Then she better be ready to ride some crazy dick." Jayce puts my craving to words.

I jab him in the side, watching his expression. "You wouldn't?"

He lets out a long breath. "I would."

"If she came over here right now?"

"Then she'd be asking for both of us. Are you going to say no?"

I turn back to the window. She's dangling her bra from her fingertips. "Why the hell was I looking at you while she was stripping?"

"Because you want a piece of this too." Jayce grabs his crotch.

I don't have to look to know the gesture, but I do. And he's right. I want both of them.

Jayce lunges away from the pool table, ripping me from the craziest thought I've ever had. He's reaching for the blinds. I focus past him. Madison's fingers are tucked into her panties, pulling them halfway down her ass.

But the blinds come down faster, the cords releasing unevenly, holding one side up several inches while the other crashes into the sill.

"What the hell?"

"It can't be like this." Jayce bangs a fist against the wall, still holding the end of the cord. His head drops against his arm.

I'm torn. I'd been testing him, making sure he was committed, but now that he put a halt to it, I'm not ready for it to end. "Can't be like what? You just said—"

"Don't tell me what I said. Give me one day. I'll figure this out."

I reach for the cord and he yanks it away. "Okay, okay. If you're afraid to come in front of me, I'll go first."

"That's not it."

"Then what is it? If I leave and find out you opened these curtains…"

"You'll what?"

I back away. "Nothing. We both have a lot to think about."

He nods slowly. "I want to sleep on it. Talk to her tomorrow."

"You know you can trust me."

He paces silently. What the hell is Madison thinking right now? Does she feel rejected? The thought makes my chest hurt.

Jayce pulls his thoughts together. "I realize Madison is just another girl to you, but I know her. And I don't think I'm going to be able to be satisfied with a few cheap thrills. I'm going after her. That's why I had to close the blinds. This isn't a strip club where we have some fun and walk away. I want her."

Jayce and I have shared some wild business ideas. We've taken risks. But nothing has felt this dangerous or this right.

"Are you willing to share?"

"I don't think she'd be satisfied with anything less. Let me sort this out tomorrow, make sure she knows what she's getting into."

Six

Jayce

Shit sure can hit the fan at the worst time. I hang up from a call with Brett. He asked if I'd go pick up the paper copy of Roarke's letter of recommendation for him. Who needs paper copies in the age of digital communication? He'll probably frame the damn thing. Be proud he got a letter of recommendation from the great Doctor Shepherd.

I agree—anything to keep my son away from Madison. And it gets me in their house, which plays perfectly into my need to talk to her.

I storm over to their house and share the details of the breakup with Roarke since he seems completely ignorant of what his daughter's been through. On other counts, I'll accept his blissful obsession with work and not knowing what his daughter's up to.

By the time I've spelled out why Madison broke my son's nose, we're in agreement that Brett deserved it. Roarke's already sent the digital copy of the letter to Brett and hands me the paper copy since he's a man of his word. And he's still caught up on the whole image thing, wants to keep things quiet.

He'd lose his mind if he knew her other secrets. Maybe it's best that she's not around. He might be able to see right through the façade I'd have to wear if she was in the room.

Roarke is monologuing about the latest programs he's brought to the hospital, and I have to admit he's an asset to the community. But having overheard Madison and Brett talk the last few years, I know his success came at a cost of not being there for her.

My urge to protect her grows with each word as he drones on.

"Oh, Madison. We were just talking about you." He interrupts his own rambling to greet his daughter who's rubbing her eyes as she comes down the stairs. Her little shorts and crop top tease my dick. *Down boy*.

"Oh no. I didn't realize we had company." She freezes mid-step. "I thought you were on the phone. Um…I forgot something in my room."

She takes a step up but her dad stops her.

"Nonsense, Madi. You need to hear what Jayce had to say. Something you should have told me earlier. And I need to make a lot more effort to get to know my own daughter."

She must guess from his tone that he doesn't know about the window.

"I really need to look over my lesson plans for next week." She takes another step up.

I don't know how I'll get a chance to talk to her if she goes back upstairs. Even if she stays downstairs, I'm not sure how I'll get her alone. I have to wing it.

"He's right. Have a seat." Can everyone hear the possessiveness in my voice? Is anyone else hoping she'll sit in my lap? I want her close enough, I can smell her subtle minty scent. So delicate but lively, just like her.

She moves cautiously down the steps.

"You defended yourself against my son, but you let your dad think you were in the wrong. Guess that means I have to stand up for you."

Her eyes go wide.

My gaze is fixed on her as she settles behind a chair. The swell of her pajama top over her breasts reminds me just how perky her tits are.

I manage to focus. "I was talking to Brett this morning when he mentioned that your father was writing a letter of recommendation for his med school application. After what happened between the two of you, I was surprised, so I came over to find out if my son was lying. He hasn't exactly been truthful lately. Even to the point of hurting the people he should care about the most."

"That's where you could have been a little more open, dear." Her dad has no idea what he's in the middle of.

"We broke up. Nothing to see."

Is she trying to tempt me with her wording? I've seen her nearly naked beauty. It's almost evil that she can be so perfect.

"Don't underestimate yourself, Madison." I notice her chest heave when I use her name. I noticed it the other night too. Does she like that?

"Have a seat, Madi. You should get to know our neighbor. I like him."

She slinks around the chair, clutching her hands in her lap.

"I like you too, Roarke. All that stuff you told me a few minutes ago about how you're proud of her standing up for herself makes me think I should get to know the real Madison, not the version my son failed to appreciate. I don't think he has any idea how badly he messed up."

My dad leans toward Jayce and smirks. "Or maybe he got out just in time. Gotta watch out for women who are willing to throw punches, you know what I mean?"

My eyes are laser-focused on Madi. "Better that she'll stick up for herself than let a guy disrespect her. A man would only have to be worried if he didn't intend to treat his woman like the gift she is."

Madison looks like she's not breathing. It's too soon to rush over and give her mouth to mouth.

"I suppose." Roarke leans back.

"Your daughter is smart, beautiful, and strong. A pretty desirable package, if you ask me." I'm straddling the line. It's not easy to make sure Roarke hears one thing while his daughter hears another.

Roarke side-eyes me and furrows his brow. "Nobody asked."

Might have gone too far. "Just pointing out that my son must be an idiot for hurting her. And I'm sorry for whatever parenting failure I made that led to that."

"Ha! We can't be responsible for everything our kids do." Back on track, Roarke is playing into my hand. It won't be easy for him to accept that I'm going to make his daughter mine, but I'll get him as ready as possible.

I nod at him. "Good point. It's hard to let them do things we don't approve of. Thanks for the reminder that we have to respect them as the adults they've become. Let them make their own mistakes, right? I bet you made a few."

Madison catches my eye, pleads with me to stop. I wink. Based on the slight drop of her jaw, she gasped. I bet her panties are getting wet too. I still can't get over how lucky I am that my son got a taste of her and let go.

Her dad laughs it off. "Mistakes were made. But if I'd listened to my parents, I wouldn't have Madi. I've earned the bad dad award plenty of times, but my life is so much better because of her. Balancing a career and a kid, as a single dad, is pretty damn hard. Sorry for learning to parent on your watch, kiddo."

Madison looks shocked. Is this the first time he's told her that? There might be a message in this for me with Brett. I'll sort that out later.

"What about you, Madison, do you want to have kids?"

That might be one of the least smooth segues ever, so I regroup. "I mean from a career standpoint. Have you thought about how all of it will work out?"

"Sure, I love kids." The innocence in her voice thickens my need to give her everything she wants.

My lips curve into a smile despite my attempt not to show excitement. I'd give her a baby tonight if I could.

She continues, "My job is most important right now, while I'm single, but I want a family, a normal life."

"Hmm…I think you need something a little different than normal. There's a fire in you. Something that won't settle for a normal guy."

She purses her lips and nods. Does she know that guy is me? Is that why she's teased me? How the hell does Elijah factor in? The three of us have something special.

"Don't get her started on how much she loves kids. It made teaching an easy choice for Madi."

"Really?" I look at Madison who's staring at me with a deer in the headlights expression, but her dad keeps rambling.

"She needs to establish her career first. If things go wrong in a relationship, she can't count on guys like us being willing to raise their own kids." Roarke is forking over valuable information.

I hope she understands what I'm doing. "I agree that she needs to be in charge of her own life, her own decisions.

It's important she thinks about her choices, and makes them carefully. Some are harder to go back from than others."

Determination settles over her. "Everything I'm doing right now is intentional. I don't intend to go back on anything."

Roarke is the only thing stopping me from scooping her into my arms, carrying her to her bedroom, and telling her I want to ride her bare.

He shakes his head. "It's easy to say when you're young, but you haven't lived. Juggling a career and a family is hard work."

"Guess hindsight's twenty-twenty when you're divorced," she sasses.

My palm itches to bend her over my knee. "There's nothing wrong with a woman wanting a career. There's also nothing wrong with wanting to raise children more than you want a career. You just need to make sure you discuss that early in a relationship. Make sure you have a man who can give you that dream. That he's someone who can properly cherish you. I had a friend over last night, Elijah, and we were just talking about this."

She visibly swallows.

"You're a smart guy, Jayce. What we want from our daughters and our wives doesn't always line up. Why haven't we hung out more? You summed up my girl... All fired up when she decides she wants something. I suppose every dad wishes for more than the average guy for his little girl. Hard to believe Brett wasn't the one." He pauses to laugh. "I'd say we need to find a good guy like Brett's dad for you, Madi."

He just threw gas on the fire. I feign nonchalance.

"Thank you, Mister Shepherd. Your opinion means a lot to me."

"Don't let it go to your head, Jayce. Every man has his faults. For you, it's that damned third story you want to put on your house. I'm still filing complaints with the city. I can't let you block my gorgeous view."

"Are you sure that's the most gorgeous view?"

"Nothing beats these mountains and the lake." He looks out the window.

I shift my attention to Madison. "Gorgeous beyond compare."

Roarke stands and extends a hand. "You're a good guy, but I'm not fooled for a second. You won't be getting that third story."

I follow his lead and keep our handshake civil. "You might be in luck. There may be something I want more. I'm going to have my business partner over again to discuss it. Good talking to you."

Resisting any kind of contact with Madison, I nod and wink at her. "Give those decisions serious thought. Then don't let anyone stand in your way."

Seven

Madison

Locking myself in my bedroom, I slump against the door, finally able to breathe. My legs are too weak to support me and I slide to the carpet.

Oh. My. God.

Did Jayce just say that he wants to cherish me and give me babies?

It was barely a week ago when Brett smashed my dream of children, or even a relationship, into a million pieces. His father just glued them all back together. In front of my dad.

The damn curtains call to me. I'd cursed them and the window and all of my bravado when Jayce closed the blinds last night. I'd wallowed in rejection. I hated him. And his son. And all men.

Now I get it. He wanted commitment. I think.

Can I be certain that's what just happened? Yes, I can.

Elijah. Jayce is a clever one. Same time, same place?

I really do need to finish setting up my classroom. School starts Wednesday, a short week. Keeping the windows closed while I get dressed, I'm caught up in how surreal my life suddenly feels.

I'll do what Jayce said and give my decision serious thought. Devoting a few hours to finish setting up my classroom will give me time for that.

The tedium of organizing books by skill level and stapling cute teddy bears with each student's name to the bulletin board allows me to consider which names I'll give our kids. I'm way past giving the relationship a yes or no. I don't even know Elijah yet, but I'm sold. This definitely clenches that I'm not wired right.

My thoughts are way too many steps ahead. I'm still a virgin.

Ouch! I staple my finger. Grabbing a Band-Aid from my desk drawer, I tend to my injury. I better focus. I can deal with the virgin thing later. It won't be a deal-breaker, will it?

Checking off task after task, I step to the doorway of my classroom and admire the bright colors, the cozy reading nook complete with a futon pad and lots of cushions, and all of the tables with students' names on placards. It's beautiful.

And it's not enough.

I toy with the teddy bear cut-outs I slipped into the pocket of my sundress. Each one contains one of the names I want to use for our kids: Marly, Max, Maya, Mason, Maggie, and Maddox.

Will Jayce and Elijah be okay with our kids' names all starting with M-a?

So many questions before we get to that.

Locking my classroom door, I imagine my students lined up in the hallway, eagerly awaiting their next lesson.

I practice my soft but authoritative voice. "Remember to keep your voices turned off. You'll have plenty of time to use them when we get to the music room and Miss Simmons teaches you a new song." With a deliberate pace appropriate for little legs, I pretend to walk my line of kiddos to the music room.

In just a few days, I'll have my instant batch of kids—not quite the same as if they're my own children, but I'm eager to be an influence in so many young people's lives. Unless of course...

I push the bar on the front door, opening it to the bright sunshine.

My heart pounds. Jayce and Elijah are waiting for me in the recessed entry.

"What are you doing here?"

I've been near Jayce many times, but ever since his hands had been around my waist, things had felt different. And ever since this morning when he revealed his intent, I'd wondered if this whole teaching thing would end sooner than I'd expected. We're alone now, with Elijah. No father to hide intent from.

This is the first time I've been in his physical presence since my embarrassing exit. The combo of the two men is like getting to pick two treats from the ice cream truck. Only the treats want to eat me. And they're super-hot instead of cold. And—

Jayce stomps toward me. Why does he look mad? I back against the door. The warmth of the sun baking into the huge chunk of metal has nothing on the heat emanating from him. He braces a hand beside my head against the door. "I expected to see you after our little chat with your dad. You don't think you can agree to be mine—"

"Ours." Elijah corrects.

"You don't think you can agree to be ours and not make good on it, do you?"

I'm pretty sure society would tell me to be offended by that kind of comment, in a deep growly voice, by a man who's towering over me acting like he's the boss of me.

But no.

Exactly the opposite. Security, desire, and devotion envelop me. This is our turning point.

I drag my eyes up the expanse of his chest, linger in the few chest hairs that peek out from above the v-cut of his fitted t-shirt, then finally make it past the stubble on his neck and chin to stagger my way up to his eyes.

They strip me of everything. My clothes, my secrets, my soul. Everything belongs to him.

Elijah presses beside Jayce, his hand on the other side of my head. How could I possibly forget he was there? I don't think I did. It's just that Jayce demanded so much of my space.

I shift my lust-addled gaze to Elijah. His eyes are a vibrant green. His hair is decidedly brown but now that we're closer, the red highlights become apparent. His lips are fuller than Jayce's. I imagine they'd feel amazing trailing over my body. Not that I have any experience there.

Caged between the school where I'll spend countless hours tending to other people's children and the two men I want to be the fathers of my own children, I lose track of the question Jayce asked.

I lose track of which man is harder or muskier or more demanding…I lose track of everything.

Next thing I know, I'm curled against a broad chest. It's darker than it was a second ago. And I'm all swoony.

"Oh crap. What happened?" I scramble to get Jayce to set me down. Why is he carrying me? How did we get inside the school?

He holds me tighter while striding down the hallway. My efforts to get free are pointless. Elijah is several paces ahead.

"You passed out." Jayce's tone is soft, full of concern. "We used your ID to open the door."

"Here it is. Miss Shepherd." Elijah's brief statement is followed by a tearing sound.

I turn to see what happened. He ripped the paper sign with my name off of the wall beside my door.

"What are you doing?"

"You're not your father's anymore. You're ours." Elijah uses my key to open my classroom and Jayce carries me in. The room shrinks around these huge men.

"But my students—"

"If you insist on working, every damn single dad in the school will know that you're ours. Miss Hampton-Carrington," Jayce says.

"Carrington-Hampton sounds better, and the students will appreciate the alphabetical order of the names." Elijah sounds a little too competitive to be taking this lightly.

Why doesn't it seem premature to let them sort this out? Why is Jayce still carrying me?

Elijah closes and locks my classroom door then returns to us, pinning me between the two of them. Jayce is doing all the work holding me, which gives Elijah the freedom to stroke a hand through my hair while the other teases over my calf.

"Are you okay?" Jayce asks.

"Yeah, sorry. I'm not sure what happened. I've been pretty overwhelmed lately. A lot of changes and...anyway, you can set me down."

"When I set you down, I'm going to be ready to make you mine. Do you understand what that means?" Jayce's eyes have gone dark again like the night I ran into him.

So many questions had swirled through my mind. Was he mad? Lustful? Confused?

The answer is now clear. That dark, feral, possessive look means sex. Elijah has it too. My insides twirl until I'm almost dizzy again. It's hard to be inconspicuous about taking deep breaths when you're clutched between two thick chests.

"What happened here?" Elijah examines the bandage on my finger.

"It's nothing. Miscued with the stapler."

Wanting to dismiss his concern and focus on the moment, I try to pull my hand from his grip to motion toward the bulletin board. He doesn't let go.

"We can't have you working a dangerous job."

"It's not that dangerous."

"What if it had been someone other than us outside the building?" Elijah does have a point.

"I'll be more careful. I promise."

"You won't have to. We'll take care of you from here on out."

Elijah nods toward my cozy reading nook. Jayce carries me over.

"I'm fine really. I don't need to rest."

"This isn't so you can rest. Remember what I said I was going to do when I set you down?" Jayce clarifies.

My breath catches. I hadn't realized he'd meant right here. Right now.

"We're giving you a lot more than our last names. That is what you want, isn't it, Madison? You didn't parade around in the window just to tease us, did you?" Elijah keeps himself in the mix.

I mentally fumble how to answer, since he asked two contradictory questions. I opt for being very clear, which is far from how my mind feels. "Yes, it's what I want. And no, not just to tease you."

"Have you been parading your sweet ass in front of us so we'd be overflowing with cum by the time we finally got to claim you?" Jayce plants a tender kiss on my lips then repositions me. I'm about to be set down, which means my secret is coming to an end.

I nod. Not exactly how I'd expected the parading to work out, but I like that he gave me credit. Which means they probably don't realize I'm a virgin. Can I keep from messing this up?

Elijah helps steady me on my feet. His lips meet mine as I surrender to the way he claims my mouth. I'm already his. If I'd have known this is what it felt like, I wouldn't have been willing to wait.

Elijah's hips press into my front as he leans to kiss me.

Warmth on the back of my thigh stirs me to realize that Jayce is behind me. Fingers tucking into my panties, slowly sliding them down my hips, give me a clue what Jayce is up to, in the tiny fraction of my brain that can still think. His breath turns to kisses, trailing over parts of my body I didn't know I wanted kissed. He massages my ass with one hand while the other slides between my legs.

Past any point of decency. Past anywhere I've been touched. Past the edge of my panties.

There's no embarrassment anymore. Their confidence makes me trust that my body is doing what it was designed to do. And I hope that ends with making a baby. Is that what they mean by making me theirs? Claiming me? I don't want to be able to walk away from this.

Their hands, their mouths, their entire beings ignite my body into a bonfire of passion and need. I drop a hand behind me. My skirt has fallen over Jayce's head. It doesn't stop me from stroking him, holding him close. Taking what's mine. Or surrendering. I can't tell anymore. My existence is intertwined with theirs.

"Oh sweet baby, you're ready for this. How long would you have made us wait if we didn't show up here?"

"I don't know." I manage between kisses.

"Lay her down." Jayce plants one last kiss on my butt cheek then lets his hands trail down the side of my legs before shoving the extra cushions out of the way.

Elijah lowers me into place. Have they talked about how this will work? I only understand the basics.

"Are you sure you're ready?"

"Yes," I whisper. Am I supposed to do something?

Jayce's large hand grips my ankle, moving it so I'm spread for him. My sundress bunches at my hips, leaving nothing to his imagination. Shots of adrenaline course through me. Will nature guide me to fake that I know what I'm doing? Will I accidentally reveal my secret? A distraction might help.

I unbutton the top button of my sundress.

"You want me to suck on those pretty titties of yours while Jayce fucks you?"

"Please." Is that too polite? I'm a mess as the shiver of excitement that runs through my body causes me to lose hold of the next button.

Elijah takes over the buttons, but Jayce's finger dragging over my slit consumes my attention.

"Damn, baby. That made you even wetter. Check this out, Elijah. If you want a taste of pure Madison, you better get it now, because I'm about to fill her up."

Should that turn me on? It does. My hips lift, pressing my back into the futon.

Elijah moves a hand to my knee and draws it out more as he leans to admire my wetness. The way they look at me takes away any wrongness. It empowers me. I can't imagine belonging to anyone but them.

"Fuck." He moves his hand from my knee to my sex, dipping two fingertips inside.

I catch my breath. I've officially been breached by a man. And if a finger feels that good...

There's no time to finish the thought when he lifts his hand to his lips and groans. It takes me a second to understand that he's inhaling my scent. Then tasting as he slides his fingertips into his mouth.

"You need dick bad, don't you baby girl?" Jayce asks.

I nod furiously.

"Are you always this needy?"

I shake my head biting my lower lip as he leans between my legs, lapping at my center. My core knots tighter than ever before. My hands clasp at pillows on either side of me. Elijah finishes my buttons, and thanks to a no-bra day, his tongue is working my nipples, sending currents of tension into the knot. I'm being wound by both men at once.

Then I shatter. My legs slam against Jayce's head. I think he laughs but I can't tell. Colors and lightness fill my world. My body doesn't exist anymore. I'm lost entirely to these two men.

I drift, like a feather, swaying between the two of them, between my old reality and my new one.

My entire body is warm. Something hard presses at my sex, and it takes me a second to realize Jayce has crawled over me. It's not his tongue between my legs anymore.

His cock presses and pulls back. Then he does it again and my naughty lips part easily with my slickness. But as he presses more the fullness starts. My secret is on the line. This is way better than fingers.

Will I be more believable if I open my eyes? I do. I'm not prepared for the pure wanton expression on Jayce's face.

The strain. The love. Yes, I'm sure I see that too. It matches everything I'm feeling.

He wraps his arms under mine, cupping his hands around my shoulders. His body is too still. I need more. My next orgasm is already craving its release. Bucking my hips, I'm instantly met with more than I expected.

It hurts, but it's good. I'm full, but I crave.

Jayce slams the rest of the way into me, pulls out, then cries out, "Fuck, baby. How are you so tight?"

"I...I..." I can't say it. I won't. I'm not anymore. Blinking through the sensation as he enters me, I meet his gaze.

He sees through me. "Fuck. Are you a virgin?"

Panic races through me. I could lie.

Instead, the stretch of my walls around his cock is too much. I can't talk. I can't stop the next climax. I'm too close. I'm too excited about getting to come on his cock.

Giving in, I buck my hips and dig my fingernails into his back. When did he get rid of his shirt? Who cares? This is what sex feels like. Wildness. Abandon. Natural perfection. My legs wrap around his best they can as I experience the most amazing feeling ever—my walls clamping around his cock. Milking him. Taking from him. Pleasing him.

"Damnit. I can't hold back." His previous question is lost to the universe as he thrusts hard, encouraging every last shred of my being to drift into bliss. Moans. Growls. Skin slapping. It becomes one with us as the mass of his body secures me against the cushion. His seed spills out of me, dripping down my ass.

Our scents join. We're mingled in every way.

I'm marked. I'm claimed. I'm happy.

And not finished...I'm reminded as Elijah struggles to talk through his urgency. He's already stripped himself from the waist down. "I need you, Madison. I need to know I have a chance of putting a baby in you today."

Jayce kisses my neck before groaning and rolling off. The emptiness of my pussy has me eager to accept Elijah and his hope for a baby.

Elijah settles between my legs as Jayce curls beside me and strokes hair from my face. His tone is tender. "I hope I wasn't too rough. I lost control when you came. Are you sure you're not a virgin?"

His question is light-hearted. He means it as a joke. Then his expression shifts. He shoves onto his elbow and holds a hand toward Elijah.

"Wait. Have you ever had sex before today?"

Lies will catch up with me, not that I can imagine him asking his son if we had sex. I shake my head.

"Madison." His voice is stern. "You should have told us. I would have been gentler."

A sob wells in my throat. I don't like him being mad at me. I angle my head away from him, suddenly feeling vulnerable.

Elijah sits back on his heels, his hand stroking my belly.

Jayce sounds frantic. "Baby, did I hurt you?"

"No." I force the word out while shaking my head.

His hand cups my chin, turning my face back to them. "Never be afraid to tell us anything."

A tear escapes and he quickly wipes it from my temple.

"Everything escalated so quickly. I wanted to know how you really are, not treat me special." I shift my gaze between both men. "Now that you know, do you still want me?"

They talk over each other, explaining that it makes what I'm giving them even more special.

Elijah braces himself over me, kissing my lips far more tenderly than before. "I'll be gentle."

"I want your hunger and passion, not tenderness."

"Are you sure?"

"I can take it."

Jayce adds, "I don't think you'll have a choice once her tight pussy clamps down. You'll lose control."

I think that's a compliment. Happiness swirls through my chest.

Elijah prods at my entrance. "Tell me if it's too much."

I can't leave him with any doubt. "I will, but remember, your swimmers have some catching up to do."

"Damn, woman." He thrusts inside.

I'm full once again. It's not as shocking as my first time, a whole minute ago, but it's new. I can't wrap thoughts around it as my next orgasm builds wickedly fast. My arms and legs wrap around him, holding on for dear life. He's wild, thrusting hard and fast after he meets my gaze assuring himself that I'm ready.

His cock swells and his groans start. This is my favorite moment in the entire world—watching a man come undone. His jaw drops open. His eyes lose focus. And his cock stretches me even more.

My hips buck and he meets them pump for pump. The slight perspiration adds to the slap of our skin. The sinful sounds fill my ears, driving me over the edge.

"Take it all, baby," He cries out, although I'm so far gone it barely registers.

I'm his. I'm theirs. And hopefully, I'm a mom.

It's complete insanity.

"Open up. Police." The angry voice coming from the doorway rips us from the afterglow.

Eight

Elijah

What the fuck? She's still tight around my cock but I pull out.

"Give us a second." Jayce throws his shirt on and rushes to the door, which only has a small window that isn't facing us. From the waist up, he's dressed.

I grab both sides of Madison's top and help cover her breasts. She's ours, and neither of us wants anyone else to see her. More importantly, we don't want her embarrassed. I'm already mad enough at these assholes for ruining our perfect moment.

Looking like she might vomit, she sits up, fastening the buttons better than my bulky fingers can. I'm an asshole for worrying that our seed will leak out of her.

"It's okay. We'll get rid of them." I hand her panties back to her. "You better put these on until we can properly take care of you."

"We need to speak to Miss Shepherd," one of the policemen explains.

The remaining color drains from Madison's face. I rub her back and calmly whisper, "I'm sure it's a misunderstanding. Someone must have seen us carry you in. Let them know you're okay."

"I'm fine." She clears her throat then says it again, louder. "I'm fine."

"Step to the door please, ma'am," the officer insists.

Her hands comb over her hair and I help tame her well-fucked silky strands. "You look fine."

Helping her to stand, I keep a hand on the small of her back. Her legs wobble and I'm not sure if it's from what we've just done, which is only a few minutes of what I plan on doing for hours with her, or if it's just the unsteadiness as she steps off the futon. Doesn't matter. I'm going to keep my hands on her the rest of my life.

Jayce rushes back to his clothes, throwing them on while they question Madison. The security camera had caught us in the entrance, and of course, showed me using Madison's ID to enter the building while Jayce was carrying her passed-out body. The after-hours security company had phoned it in.

She explains, "I was setting up my classroom and friends were meeting me afterward. Thankfully they were here, because when I stepped outside, I got dizzy. They brought me back in."

Fair enough. Our sexy little vixen handles it beautifully. The slight waver of her voice could easily be explained by having passed out.

"We're going to need you to open the door." On the one hand, this cop is starting to piss me off. On the other hand, if she insists on working here, it's reassuring to know the security team is attentive.

I scan the classroom for cameras. Guess she would have pointed out if there were any. Not sure what I would have done if a security guard had watched us take our virginal, soon-to-be bride.

Madison buys enough time for Jayce to get dressed then opens the door. I embrace her from behind and she clutches my forearms. My heart melts but we still have to get rid of the officers. They both enter, assessing the situation, and one of them steps toward the sex den. Cushions can hide the wet spot, but not the smell.

Officer Ortiz, according to his name tag, motions to Jayce and me, "Will the two of you step into the hallway for a minute with Officer Greer?"

I don't move.

"Sir. We need to speak to Miss Shepherd alone."

Her body shakes. Letting her go is the last thing I want to do. Does she fucking look like she's resisting? I glance down and her body is pinned against mine. Yeah, it's a toss-up. I could see how they'd be concerned.

"They're just going to make sure you're safe," I say to the top of her head and leave a kiss. Then I face my friend. "Let's go."

Officer Greer separates us in the hallway and blocks the door.

I count my breaths to convince myself that eternity doesn't actually pass. Then the door opens and Madison rushes to me. I'm closer, but let it swell my ego.

Jayce joins us, and in the background, the officers thank us and leave.

Nothing else matters besides having Madison in our arms. "You okay?"

"That was embarrassing. His son is going to be in my class."

I wish she was kidding. He asked her to get the classroom cleaned up before the kids show up. We promise to help. For now, we get her home where we can have more privacy.

There's a brief debate about who's home we'll go to but ultimately decide on Jayce's since I drove, which means less shuffling, and we can easily drop Madison's car at her house.

Nine

Jayce

Elijah insists she ride with him and I drive her car. How can such a short time away from her weigh so heavily?

They have to wait for me at my door while I park her car at her house. Seeing them together eagerly awaiting me does my heart good.

I wrap an arm around her waist and give her a kiss before unlocking the door.

She and Elijah are both comfortable in my home and I like having them under my roof. It's where we belong. I'll have to talk to them about that later.

Grabbing drinks, I meet them on the couch when she returns from the bathroom. We squeeze her in between the two of us.

"How are you doing?" I'm worried I was too rough with her, although frustratingly short-lived. Next time will be better. Elijah hadn't lasted much longer, so I don't feel like too much of a chump.

"I had no idea it would feel so good."

"It will be even better next time. I promise."

"How?"

Elijah adds, "He's right. You threw us a curveball with the virgin thing. Next time we'll take our time. There's so much to teach you."

She giggles innocently.

"Did you and Brett really never have sex?" It's a serious question. I'd always assumed my son was sexually active...with her.

Madison ducks her head. "No."

"It's okay. It was wrong of me to assume. I don't know what's wrong with that boy."

Elijah strokes Madison's arm. "His loss is our gain."

"I'll say. I tried to deny my feeling for you for years, Madison. When you left for college, I hoped that would finally be my chance to escape the spell you had on me, but I woke up with my cock in my hand far too many times."

She drags a finger over my lengthening dick. "Really?"

I angle her face up so I can kiss her plump lips. "Almost every night. And when I held you in my hands for those brief seconds the night you caught Brett cheating, I wasn't sure I could let you go."

"You shouldn't have. I've wanted you all along." She turns to Elijah. "And I wish I would have met you sooner."

He strokes a hand over her cheek and kisses her. "The important thing is that we're all together now. It's new territory for all of us. If you ever feel nervous about something...or want to try something, just say the word."

"Okay." She stands up, her smile a combination of sly and mischievous. "Who wants to go first?"

"For what?" I ask.

"I want to sit on your lap...naked."

"Fuck, yeah," I shuck my pants so fast, the two of them are left staring at my erection. "Hop on."

"Calm down, man." Elijah shakes his head then takes her hand and helps her sit on my lap, my cock standing in front of her.

He says, "If you're sore, we can wait."

"Wait to feel that good again? No thanks. I've waited too long already. Can we please try this position?" She wiggles her hips on my lap and a bead of pre-cum forms on my tip.

"I'll never deny you sex." I bunch her skirt, prompting her to raise her arms.

Elijah gets up and helps remove her dress. She's bare-ass naked on my lap.

"What happened to your panties?" I slap her ass.

"They were a mess. I threw them away in your bathroom."

I nod at Elijah. "Make a note that we need to keep panties stocked for her. I don't want her running around in public without them, but it might be hard keeping her in a clean pair with as wet as she gets."

"Can do. Want me to start some music before I grab the souvenir panties out of the trash?"

"Yes please, to the music. Maybe not on retrieving my underwear."

He grins at her wickedly as he starts a song with a strong beat. "You're about to be too busy riding dick to be worried about what I do or don't do."

She looks down at my cock, dragging a finger through the bead. Her eyes lift to mine.

I nod. "It's okay, baby. Have all the fun you want."

Inching herself up my thighs, her curls press into my cock. I can't believe she's ours. We can teach her everything, be everything. Care for her. I never considered this type of relationship, and can't quite figure out how it happened, but it's perfect.

"I was hoping you would stay here. We can all be together."

Elijah leans down, takes her in an open-mouth kiss, showing off as his tongue slides in. Her nipples bead under my fingers and my lap is wet under her pussy. What a fucking angel. I watch the two of them, and it's beautiful. She's right. He needs to join us.

When he pulls away, he says, "You two get started. Go ahead and have an orgasm on his cock, because when I get back from stealing your underwear, I'm going to take you off of his lap and set you on mine."

He rubs her hand over the obvious strain in his pants. My cock twitches. I'm not sure who's more excited about him getting back. I liked watching him fuck her earlier. Can't wait to see it again.

"Take all the time you need," I tease.

"You plan on being more than a Fast Freddy this time?" Elijah can't resist.

"Bastard," I call out as he leaves the room.

Gripping Madison's hips, I ask, "You sure you're not too sore?"

"Nothing I can't deal with."

"We'll give you a bath later, help you relax."

She pouts, which warrants another swat of her ass. I like the way she giggles and flinches when I spank her. Bet it will feel even better when she's riding my cock.

Easing her onto my shaft, I show her how she can tilt her hips, pump up and down, or hold still and let me move.

Her hands rest on my shoulders and she has trouble keeping her eyes open. Slaps to her ass make her pussy contract and her nipples tighten. They also channel her straight to orgasm.

When her breaths even out, I ask, "Want to turn around, see how a different position feels?"

"Don't you need to come?"

"I will baby. Every stroke of your pussy on my dick is like heaven."

She notices that Elijah's been gone for a few minutes so I let her in on what I suspect he's doing. "Guys never want to blow their load right away. He's probably jacking off to ease some of his need. Don't worry, one look at you and he'll be rock hard again, with better hang time though."

Helping her spin around, I balance her by holding her waist. She bounces on my cock, her youth and vigor playing to her advantage. For me, it's all about stamina and teaching my little princess how she should be treated.

Watching her ass jiggle as she takes my dick, I'm closer and closer to release. "Can I show you something?"

"Anything." Her breaths are growing heavy. She has to be nearing release.

I want to drive this one home. Easing a hand between her legs, I find her clit and rub. Her head drops back, her hair falling farther down her back, her ass rippling with each gasp as I impale her sweet pussy.

She's mine. She's ours. My heart is so full. Just like my balls.

I fist her hair, keeping her head tugged back. I wish I had a picture of her splayed on my lap while she flies impossibly close to ecstasy. I'll have to get Elijah to film us some time.

The pulse of her walls around my cock drags my release from me. Streams of cum shoot inside of her. It's already dripping onto my lap when she breaks.

I'm only faintly aware that Elijah says something.

"Jayce, oh my god." Her hand clasps over mine as her body lurches forward, her hair slipping from my fingers.

I force my eyes open so I can regrasp it, pull her back into my chest, but my gaze settles past her, across the room...on Brett.

His camera is in his hand.

Elijah throws a pillow in front of Madison and I catch it, holding it in place, knowing it's not doing enough.

"Get the fuck out of here," I yell, clutching Madison to my chest.

Madison must open her eyes. She wiggles to get away but I hold her close. There's nowhere to hide. My asshole son just needs to be a decent human being and look away. He never wanted her when he had her. It's too late now.

I grab a throw blanket from the other end of the couch and drape it in front of Madison while her pussy continues to milk the last of my seed.

Elijah storms to the doorway where Brett hasn't moved and stands between us. He'd be more intimidating if he had pants on. I can't imagine what's going through Brett's mind, or Madison's.

"I'm sorry, baby. I'll get rid of him."

Elijah backs Brett onto the porch and closes the door.

I make sure she's wrapped in the blanket, then pull my pants up.

Rage burns through me that once again we've been interrupted. Once again, she's going to do something besides let my seed take hold and put a baby in her. Once again, I have to spend a second away from her.

"I'll be right back."

"I'm so sorry." She's scrambling to get her dress on.

I grab her upper arms, hold her so she has to look into my eyes. "It's not your fault."

"He had his phone out. What if he took a picture?" Her chin quivers.

"I'm sure it was coincidence, but I'll make sure." I hug tightly. "It'll be okay."

With her slightly put at ease, I tell Elijah to get back inside and I deal with my son.

"Give me your phone." I extend my hand.

"Too late." He laughs and reaches to slip it in his back pocket.

My son may be a cocky-ass med student, but he's forgetting his place.

I step closer. Our stares lock, a face-off. Now is not the time for him to cross me, or Madison. I've failed to teach him how to treat a woman, and I'll own that. He has no excuse for not being a decent human being, though.

I pace my words. "Give me your phone."

"Worried I got a picture? Your secret will get out? How long has that been going on?" Brett looks over my shoulder.

Mint wafts over me as I realize Madison is in the doorway.

"Don't fight. It's all my fault." The worry in her voice makes me boil with rage. I remind myself this is my son. I've been at odds with him for years. His mother planted seeds against me that were hard to combat. That's why I'd been sure the only reason he chose to live with me was because of Madison.

"None of this is your fault, Madison. Go inside." My palm is no longer open for Brett to put his phone in my hand. A balled fist takes its place and if Madison hadn't just stopped me, I might have forced the issue.

My son smirks. "Fault...no, but this is even better than I had planned."

She steps beside us. Damnit. I don't want her anywhere near my scumbag son. When she shrugs off Elijah's attempt to put his arm around her shoulders, he positions himself between Madison and Brett.

I grab the phone to keep myself from shattering his face. I have to fix this for my baby girl.

"Don't forget that I still pay for this." I hold the phone up.

"Doesn't matter. Doctor Shepherd now knows that his perfect little girl has a dirty secret."

"What?" she shrieks.

"Med school's hard. Got to do what it takes to get ahead, right Dad? Isn't that your business mantra?"

"Cheating and blackmail have never been my mantra."

"Do your best, and then some. Be shrewd. No way I would have put up with Madi so long if her daddy wasn't one of the top doctors in the nation, which you made sure I knew from the moment I said I wanted to be a doctor."

My hands fly to my son's neck so fast his phone is still in my hand. I have him pinned against one of the deck columns before I can see anything but red. His fingers claw against my arms.

How dare he use Madison. How dare he twist my words.

"Stop!" Madison pleads.

I glance to the side. The hurt in her eyes is geared toward me as Elijah restrains her.

Everything is wrong. Devastation forces my hands from Brett's neck.

"I'm sorry, Madison. He's twisting my words. I never meant for him to use you or hurt you."

Tears stream down her face and Elijah's hold on her loosens. A distance has grown between us, even as she's marked by my release from moments before. Possibly carrying my baby. My world is falling apart.

"I have to make sure my dad doesn't get that message." She shrugs from Elijah's grasp and runs, taking all of the air in the world with her.

Elijah slams a hand across my chest when I start to follow. "You won't help anything by going."

I grab his wrist and shove his arm away. Turning to my son, I ask, "Did you send that picture?"

"You're the one holding the phone." Brett continues to rub his neck and take the occasional staggered breath.

His phone is locked. I grab his hand. Elijah rushes forward, ready to break us up, but I press Brett's thumb to the screen and let go.

"Keep him away from me," I direct Elijah, then move to the other side of the deck. Opening the text message, sure enough, the last one he sent is to Doc Shep. A photo's attached. My stomach sinks.

"Thanks to you, I've got leverage for keeping Doc in my back pocket."

"For what?"

"Doc wouldn't want this picture of his daughter to get out. It's my backup plan. Just in case."

"You can't just use people."

"Why not? You and mom do?"

"What on earth do you mean?"

"She said you used her to get through med school so she used you until a better offer came along. And you've never been into the dad thing. You just used me to look like a hard-working single dad."

"I may not have been a good dad, but you got it all wrong."

"Whatever."

My thumb hovers over the screen. How did I go so wrong that my son would stoop to this?

My heart beats in my throat, making it hard to breathe. Hard to swallow the guilt I carry as Brett's parent.

I have to know if the picture is what I think it is. Clicking the message, the crystal-clear photo fills the screen. It should be the most sensual thing I've ever seen. A piece of art I would hang in my private study. An intimate moment to be treasured.

Instead, it's anger, fear, and loss. Of Madison. Of our threesome. Of Madison's relationship with her father. Of Brett.

I'm crushed. There's no time to grieve. I have to fight for the things that are most important.

With Elijah's prompting, I give Madison time to clear out her dad's phone, and I attempt to untangle Brett.

But when he's in no mood to listen, I head next door.

Ten

Madison

I rush home. It's more than just to get my dad's phone before he does. I'm broken.

The tears streaming down my face cause my fingers to struggle with the numbers on our keypad.

I try again.

How could Brett do that? Was he acting on what his dad taught him? Did both of the Hamptons use me? And Elijah?

Love at first sight is nothing but a girlish fantasy. I handed myself to them on a silver platter and they ate like kings. I rub my hands over my face before I type the code into our door for the third time.

The green light flashes and the lock clicks. With no sign of dad downstairs, I run up to his bedroom. It's empty. I slump onto his bed.

Is he at the hospital making the world a better place while his spoiled daughter dabbles in depravity? He'll be so disappointed.

How can I convince him not to open the message? I fuss with the pocket in my skirt, trying to retrieve my phone.

I dial my dad. This is going to hurt. Later, if there's any chance that Calli will listen, I really need her. Rock bottom looms in my future as I wait for my dad to answer.

I swap the call to speakerphone and pull up my text messages. Maybe Calli will offer a shoulder to cry on. I don't even care if she pulls the old 'I told you so'.

I'm typing my plea to Calli, my need to talk to a friend, but pause when my dad answers.

"Hey, Madi." My dad sounds groggy. Sometimes he takes naps at the hospital.

"Dad, where are you?"

"What's wrong, Madi?"

The worry in my voice is clear to both of us.

"You're going to get a message from Brett. Please don't open it. Wherever you are, I'll come and delete it. Just don't look at it."

I decide against explaining more in my text message to Calli, and hit Send.

"I'm busy...at the hospital. I didn't see a message..."

I don't know what else he says because what I first perceive as chatter in the background becomes clearer. Minions jabbering.

Then it sounds like he's covered his phone. What the fuck? Why is Calli at the hospital? Is my dad lying?

After a pause, he's back on. "Madison?"

I pull myself together. "Sorry I got distracted. Promise me you won't open the message."

"I won't, but you need to tell me what's going on."

How awkward am I about to make things? "I'll meet you at the hospital in twenty minutes."

"No. Don't do that. I'm already on my way home."

If my dad's driving, he won't be opening messages. I should be okay with this. I should encourage him. But I have to know.

I send Calli another message: *are you with my dad?*

Minions answer the question.

"Thanks, Dad. I'll be waiting." I hang up. It's hard to process. Calli and my dad? Ew, I scurry off the bed. Have they had sex there? I shudder at the thought and head onto the deck, the one that faces away from the Hamptons.

I'm begging the stars for answers, guidance, support...anything, when distant giggling draws my attention to the mayor's house across the way. Aria's flung over some guy's shoulder. That wouldn't be remarkable in itself. What makes my heart ache is the other guy slapping her ass. Seriously? Am I the only one who can't find love?

I drop my head. If I crawl into a closet, I should be able to hide from the world while I sort my thoughts.

"Madison." Jayce is rushing to my front door but detours to the steps when he sees me on the second-story deck. I only have a few seconds to get inside.

"I learned my lesson. Leave me alone." My heart races as I dash inside and lock the huge glass doors. Along with the view through the wall of windows, it's clear that he's made it onto the deck. I hide in the safety of my bedroom.

Curtains closed. No temptation to open them ever again.

I crash onto my bed, leaning into the headboard, and curling my legs up. Did my years in a nearly platonic relationship with Brett stunt my formative relationship years? How can I fall so easily?

Maybe the other school district I'd been interested in working for hasn't filled the first-grade teacher position. I want to get as far away from here as possible. Or at least a reasonable drive away…I'll take anywhere that has a teaching position open.

I half-heartedly search on my phone.

Why didn't Calli say something? I can't focus on the listings.

"Madison?" Jayce's voice comes from inside the house.

Shit. How did he get in?

Can I protect myself when I long for the protection his arms give me? I don't have time to decide when my bedroom door flies open.

I press against my headboard. Fight or flight fails me. I'm incapable of either.

Eleven

Jayce

"Madison. Don't ever run off like that again." The words are out of my mouth the second I see her. Before I process the hurt in her expression.

"Stop." The forcefulness of her voice surprises me. I stop in the doorway.

I raise my hands. "I'm sorry you got caught in the middle of that. I can't believe my own son would stoop so low. I deleted the picture from his phone and where he saved it on the cloud. But..."

I rub my temples. It pains me to admit the rest.

Her voice is softer but unsettled. "I made my dad promise not to open it. I'm going to delete it from his phone when he gets home. I'll handle it. Please leave."

"Baby. No. I can't stand to see you like this. Can't stand that I'm in any way responsible for your pain." I also can't stand in the doorway any longer. I stride to her bed, ignoring her protest.

The bed sinks under my weight, giving me the advantage of throwing Madison off balance. I loop my hand around her waist and pull her against me. She's in my arms. I can breathe again.

Her body accepts me, but her words hold me at bay. "You don't have to pretend to care. I'll get rid of the picture. I don't want anyone to see it any more than you do."

"Pretend? You can't believe what Brett said. He turned my words, my intent into something ugly. I never would advocate him hurting you to advance his career. I don't understand what got into him. If I'd known he was using you, I would have stopped him. I've loved you for longer than I should admit. I've sacrificed my happiness for my son's."

"You have?" She squirms to face me.

I stroke my thumb over her tear-stained cheek. "I've never been able to convince myself that I don't love you. Giving you my...our last names isn't a joke. And I promise to be a better dad for our children than I was with Brett." It's taking all of my willpower not to take her right here on her bed, but since her dad is on his way home, I have to wait.

"You're serious?"

"The night you broke up with Brett, I wanted to claim you right there in the hallway, but you looked so hurt and broken...betrayed, by my son. I told myself that the look of desire that flashed through your expression was my imagination. I had to give you time. A few nights later, you stopped the clock."

"And Elijah? Have you had a relationship with him before?"

"Never. I can't explain how we both felt right about sharing you. He'd be here now if I hadn't asked him to keep Brett under control. I tried talking to my son, but he refused. I'll try again later."

Holding her isn't enough. Knowing she's safe isn't enough. Possibly having created a life with her isn't enough. I need to be inside of her again...need to be one with her. And I need Elijah to be a part of it. He completes us.

Shifting Madison onto her back, I brace myself on my elbow and trail my hand down her body. Brett didn't hurt her physically but I still check.

Is she still mine, ours? Can she trust me the way I trust her? I need confirmation from her soul.

Our eyes lock as I caress my hand over her cheek. "I'll never let anything bad happen to you again."

"It wasn't your fault."

"Elijah and I claimed you as ours. If anything happens to you, it's our fault." I slowly lower my lips to hers. My kiss is tender, just a brush, asking if she can trust us again. Her body won't lie.

I take a breath before pressing my lips to hers again. It's wrong to do this without Elijah but I have to know.

She parts her lips, and I have my answer. She's ours forever and ever.

My cock strains against my jeans as I roll on top of her. My heart aches with the need to make everything right. I will soon enough. For now, the best I can do is to be close.

"I love you so much, Madison."

"Madi? Where are you?" Her dad's words inch through the storm in my brain. I can't convince myself to move. She's not moving. Did I make it up?

"Get the hell off my daughter." Roarke is running across the room by the time I lift my head.

Instinct drives me into action. I'm off the bed, grabbing the punch Roarke is ready to throw.

"Madi, are you okay?" Her dad asks, leaning to look around me.

"I'm fine, Dad. He's my boyfriend."

A huff with the word 'husband' comes from my chest.

Roarke narrows his gaze at me and backs off. "What the hell is going on?"

Madison's on her knees on the bed. I back against the mattress and put my arm around her. I'm about to explain that I'm in a relationship with his daughter, but as I fumble for a way to say it that might put him at ease, Madison addresses the other problem, making me an asshole for forgetting.

"Dad, give me your phone."

"Get your hands off my daughter." His gaze remains fixed on me. I do the right thing and help her shuffle to stand then remove my hands. Elijah was right. I'm not helping.

"Please tell me you didn't open the message."

He lifts his phone from his pocket but when she grabs it, he doesn't let go. "I was going to, but Cal—"

He freezes. Madison freezes. I'm not sure what the big deal is.

Worry etches his face. Madison yanks again, and this time the phone slides free.

"You were with her, weren't you?" She doesn't immediately open his messages. What am I missing? Who was Roarke with?

He lowers his head and rubs a hand over his mouth. "Madison, we were going to tell you."

She stiffens her spine. "So don't judge me for my relationship."

I like where this is going even though it pains me that I'm not the one standing up for my girl. Damn this relationship shit is hard. Mentioning Elijah should probably happen at a different time.

Her dad shoots a warning look my way.

"We're together, Roarke. I love Madison." I close the distance between myself and my girl, staking my claim with my arm around her waist.

He doesn't look happy, but he also doesn't object. Whoever Madison called her dad out for having a relationship with worked.

She opens his phone, goes straight to the messages, and when the photo opens, she pauses. It's impossible to guess everything that's going through her mind, but she has to see how absolutely breathtaking she is.

Then, with two clicks, the photo is gone.

Instead of handing the phone back, she deletes the entire message thread between Roarke and Brett. Turns out they've talked quite a bit. It's like I barely know my own son. How much of that is on me?

I have to do better by everyone moving forward.

"What could it have been that you had to delete it?" Roarke reaches for his phone but she twists to the side.

"You really didn't look?" She's surprised.

"You asked me not to?"

"But you and Brett are so buddy-buddy."

"You're my daughter. I'd do anything for you." His words hit home for me. I'd do anything for my son...albeit, not choking him when he hurt my girl is a far cry from not opening a text message. But understanding sinks in. I have to make things right with Brett, get to the bottom of why he's gone off the deep end.

"Thanks." The timidness of her response speaks volumes.

I watch over her shoulder as she opens his contacts and deletes Brett's name. Can't say that I blame her. But I don't understand why she scrolls down more, stopping in the C's. She scrolls up and down, not seeming to find whatever she's looking for.

"Madi, I'm sorry I wasn't around much and for ever making you think I cared about Brett more than you. And that I didn't ask why you punched him. And for not simply trusting you."

"Do you now?"

Maybe a few good things came from my son being an asshole. This tender moment between father and daughter is teaching me lessons. How many times have I sat with Brett and listened to him? How many times have I bonded with him instead of making sure he's versed in how to get ahead in life? Those lessons went seriously wrong.

"As you figured out...I was with Calli when you called. We can talk about that later. But when I hung up with you, I was going to open the message from Brett. It was Calli who made me realize that if you were that upset, I needed to respect your wishes. She's the one who reminded me how important you are to me." He swallows hard. "I had to be reminded. I'm so sorry."

Calli. Not sure who that is, but that must explain who Madison was looking for on his phone. Don't think I recall seeing that name.

"Okay."

"And no offense, Jayce." Roarke shifts his focus to me. Adrenaline flows as if I'm being intimidated by my girlfriend's father rather than talking to my neighbor.

I stand taller and nod. "I'm going to get to the bottom of whatever is wrong with my son."

"Good luck. He's going to be pretty mad at me. I'm revoking my letter of recommendation. I'll be letting my peers at the med school he's applying to know that I don't advocate accepting him."

"Some of the best lessons are learned the hard way." The statement is just as much for myself and the wake-up call I needed for parenting my grown son.

"Because he cheated on me?" Madison sounds more surprised than ever.

Roarke shakes his head. "That's only part of it."

She shrugs. "What else?"

"I don't know what was in that text message. And you don't have to tell me." He waves a hand between us, highlighting his point. "You are the epitome of kindness, Madi. Anything he would send me that would hurt you reveals grievous character flaws. Being a doctor requires trust and compassion and discretion, which Brett seems to be lacking."

Madison rushes forward, flinging her arms around her dad's neck. When's the last time I hugged my son. When's the last time I complimented him on who he is rather than what he's achieved? Fuck, I have a lot of work to do...as long as it's not too late.

Nervous energy fills me but I can't leave.

"Everything I did, pushing you to have a career, to be able to take care of yourself, to want to be more than a mom, was meant to protect you. My long hours at the hospital were part of that. I wanted to make enough money that I could give you everything you deserved." Her dad's setting a damn good example, but now that they're made up, there are other issues.

"Being a single parent is pretty fucking hard, Roarke." I pull my girl back from him and she folds naturally against me.

"By the time we see our mistakes, our kids are grown." He gives Madi a weak smile.

"You don't have to worry about this one anymore." I hug her closer. "We've got her from here."

Madison's body goes rigid.

"We?" Roarke asks, about the same time I realize my slip.

Madison starts to explain but I pull her into me and take over. "There's more to our relationship than just Madison and me. A friend of mine, Elijah Carrington, is a part of it. I'm sure that's hard to swallow, but I promise that he loves your daughter—"

"You don't have to explain. Well, you do, but probably not the part you think you need to."

"What?" Madison asks.

"Calli and I are together." Roarke brings the name up again.

"Yeah. It's weird and icky that you're dating my friend but I guess I'm not in a place to judge."

"I didn't realize who she was until I'd fallen for her."

Hell, that took a turn, but Roarke has more to say.

He paces away from us and exhales hard. "Do you remember my friend Bennett Grey?"

"Yeah." Madison must be drawing the same conclusion as I am. Is there something in the water? Can threesomes be contagious?

"Well..." Stress etches itself all over Roarke's expression.

As much as I want him to grovel to his daughter, I can win some strategic points by helping him with the reveal. "The three of you? Is that what you're trying to say?"

"Yeah. I should have told you sooner, Madison."

She shivers, but this should make things immensely easier.

"It's okay. I just wish you or Calli would have told me. Can we finish this conversation later?"

Her dad agrees.

I'm considering telling Roarke that I won't have the third story built on my house if he'll give his blessing, but Madison isn't an object to be negotiated.

"Let's go see if Brett's ready to offer you a few apologies, and let Elijah know that we have your father's blessing." I wink at her dad and I'm pretty sure he hides a cringe. I'm not really waiting for his blessing, so I whisk Madison back to my house. Brett can apologize or leave, for now. But Madison won't be disrespected in my house ever again.

I can't see a scenario where he'd be willing to stay, but I'll make a game plan to be a better part of his life. To understand how he got to this point.

Epilogue

Elijah

I show the photographer, Mary, the game room we've converted into a sex den. Madison was into a lot more than window exhibitionism. Every toy or piece of furniture we tried, she liked, so we had to make a room for her to play.

"I can see why you booked three hours for the photo shoot. There's a lot to work with here." She smiles while surveying the room, not at all uncomfortable with our toys.

Madison had been given a recommendation for Mary by the mayor's daughter. She'd done a sexy photo shoot with her stepbrothers. I didn't ask questions, just ran with the recommendation. Moving into Jayce's house, with all of his history with Madison, I sometimes felt like an outsider.

This photo shoot is my way of securing my mark on the house. I'm pretty sure I've already marked her. I'd bet money the baby in her belly is mine. Just a feeling, but even if it's not, watching her belly grow makes me the happiest man alive.

Her attention is caught by the six paper teddy bears on the table. "What's this?"

"When Madison was setting up her classroom, she made those for the names she wanted to use for her own kids."

"I didn't realize she was a teacher."

"She's not. She got a better offer." I wink then guide Mary across the room. "This will be the trickier part. I first met Madison through that window. That used to be her bedroom." I motion to her former window. "I want you to capture her doing a strip tease from there."

She grimaces. "I'll need her consent."

"That won't be a problem. She's an adventurous one, thus the room. In fact, I think I just heard them." I call for them to come up.

Madison and Jayce give the photographer a curious look when they enter the room. I do introductions and explain what I have planned. And before I know it Madison is in her old window, her silky robe caught on her elbows, leaving her shoulders, swollen breasts, and beautiful belly bare. Six months gives her an undeniable bump.

I lean against a chair that's near the window and Jayce leans against the spanking bench.

The pool table is long gone, gave it to the neighbors. Madison had let it slip that she'd fantasized about having sex on it, but Jayce and I knew that fantasy had been when she was with Brett. It didn't matter that she wasn't having sex with Brett, and she swore the fantasy had been of Jayce…it made him uncomfortable. He doesn't like the overlap of when his son dated Madison. He's still working on his relationship with Brett and they're on the right track, it's reasonable that there are still issues for both of them.

The photographer is hard at work.

Jayce shifts as if trying to conceal his cock straining against his pants. I step beside him, resting a hand on his thigh.

"She's cool," I say, no idea if I'm quiet enough that the photographer doesn't hear. She continues to capture images of Madison. The pregnancy will be documented along with every bit of our love for her, and each other.

He rubs a hand over his cock. "I'm not used to anyone seeing us."

"Don't be shy. You've got a gorgeous cock." I ease my hand over the front of his slacks. He's ridiculously hard already. Nerves aren't giving him stage fright.

He clamps a hand over mine, gripping his shaft harder, and narrows his gaze at me. He whispers, "I'm not sure about this photo shoot."

A flash draws my attention to the photographer who's turned to us. "That's one hell of a hot pose."

I bet it is. We're side by side, our cocks tenting our pants, our heads turned to one another. I can't wait to see the photo.

Madison's window is dark. We must have missed her finishing. Until she gets back here, we might as well have some fun.

I say quietly, "They're just pictures. We'll delete any you don't like."

Turning sideways, I tuck my finger into Jayce's belt. "What do you say?"

He nods.

I loosen Jayce's belt, slide it from around his waist, and hand it to him. His jaw flexes. I unfasten his pants, only dropping the zipper part way.

He scowls at me. My balls tighten. He loves control, but he also likes being pushed.

The photographer continues working. When Madison enters, I motion for her to join us. "I think Jayce would feel better about this if you were by his side."

She kisses each of us and stands on the other side of him. We've pretty much done every combination of us together, but Jayce is right. It's different with a photographer. Perhaps it's easier for me because I set it up, but he's not shying away.

And Madison's become quite the exhibitionist.

She drags a finger over the belt. "Getting started without me?"

Jayce wraps the leather around her ass, pulling her to straddle his leg best she can. "I saw you slide your fingers into your pussy."

"Who me?" she teases.

Jayce loops the leather around her right wrist and uses the restraint to guide her fingers to his nose, then mine.

"What do you think, Elijah. Did she play with herself?"

"There's one way to know for sure." I put my hand over the belt, holding her fingers close so I can suck on them. Then I ease Madison off his leg and lean her against the chair.

Releasing his hand and the belt, I say, "Hold onto her. I'm going to be a while."

The stress has left Jayce's expression. The photographer moves around the room but we're with each other and I suspect that's what puts him at ease.

I drop to my knees, grab Madison's thighs, shove them apart, and lap at her pussy which has grown sweeter with the pregnancy. I can't see what's going on above, but I can tell she's angled her body a little sideways. I lift her leg over my shoulder to help.

Remembering that I had a task, I kiss my way over to her thigh, drawing a frustrated moan from her. "She definitely had her fingers in her pussy."

Jayce huffs a laugh but is clearly distracted.

It's not until I've made my assessment that her fingers bore the evidence of where they'd been that I look around her belly.

The belt around her neck almost makes me blow my load. It's just looped, not tightened, but he's holding both ends just above her breasts, pulling her in for a deep kiss. No wonder he sounded distracted.

With the two of them side by side, I snake a hand up to his cock and rub over his pants while I resume eating pussy.

I could spend the rest of eternity on my knees with them, but we only have three hours for the photo shoot.

First step, give Madison an orgasm. I add a finger inside of her, making it impossible for her to hold off. Her hand tangles in my hair. Her legs buckle, and I have to move my hand away from Jayce's throbbing cock to hold her.

The rush of her release coats my face as she cries out. Jayce shifts beside her and I can't tell what he's doing until her cries are muffled. He's claimed her mouth. He loves doing that, swallowing her moans, her cries, her pleasure.

The picture is in my mind. He has both hands clasped around her head. Usually he does...with the belt it might be different. I hope he tightened his grasp. She looked so hot with the black leather around her neck.

Easing her through the waves of release, bathed in her scent, my shirt drenched, I sit back on my heels.

They're the most sensual sight I've ever seen. And yes, he's curled the belt around his hand so it's tighter around her neck.

I stand and lower Jayce's pants while he continues to tongue fuck our sweet girl. He lifts his feet, helping me strip him bare from the waist down. Then I get naked and take my place on the fuck chair that's nearby. It's designed with lots of curves so one of us can sit in it and be straddled by someone else and joined by another...very intentionally designed for sex.

"Bring her over here." I grab the lube we keep handy and coat my cock. I'll take her ass this time, let Jayce enjoy that pussy I just got ready.

He walks her over, stopping next to the chair to kiss her again. I have to grab her hips to back her into position since they're busy making out still. The belt around her neck has my cock harder than normal, which I didn't think was possible.

"I like being able to keep you close." His voice is husky.

"Like I'd ever go very far from either of you."

"I mean really close." He steps in, towering over her, instead of waiting for her to sink onto my cock.

His hand isn't visible to me anymore but as my tip prods against her hole, my eyes close. We know this routine. But we've never had it captured on film.

She seats herself, resting on me. I'll do the work, pumping my hips under her, once Jayce gets into her soaked cunt.

It always seems like nothing can feel better than being inside of her...until Jayce is inside of her too.

"We're always best when we're together. I love you."

Jayce starts thrusting, slowly, making sure we're balanced. There are tables on either side so he can brace himself. "I'm going to miss being able to do this pretty soon."

"I'm sure we'll find a way. You can go faster. I'm good."

We always wait for her to get situated. Neither of us can imagine what it feels like to be full of so much cock and a baby.

Adding my thrusts with Jayce's we get our rhythm.

"Fuck," I hear a soft voice say, and remember the photographer. We must be quite a sight.

I glance at her. She's lowered the camera but rushes it up, resuming the photos when I catch her.

"Sorry, I've never seen anything so beautiful."

"Wait until you see her come like this," I say.

Jayce must pull her up with the belt because her head drops back as her chest moves closer to him. His lips are back on hers. His free hand is behind her back. My hands are on her hips.

And finally, I'll leave my mark on this room. When I hang these photos on every wall, any memories that have been had in the previous iteration of this room will be covered. The room will fully be ours. Everywhere we look, we'll be reminded that we belong to each other.

Madison's cries peak and I'm vaguely aware of the photographer moving to an angle where she can capture Madison's face as she climaxes.

I lose myself in her, my world obliterated as I fill her with my seed.

A second later, Jayce does the same. I don't know whose cum is dripping onto my lap, and I don't care. I'm warm. I'm sated. I'm home.

And we live happily ever after!

I hope you enjoyed **Claimed by my Ex's Dad & His Friend**, and that you're looking forward to hanging out in Eggplant Canyon for a while longer!

A bonus scene for this story is available exclusively to newsletter subscribers. If you want to find out if babies turn the Hampton-Carrington's, or is it the Carrington-Hampton's, lives upside down, you'll want this little extra. And once you're subscribed to my newsletter, I'll keep you up to date on the Super Hot stories I love to write, along with other content you won't want to miss!

Sign up at: https://SylvieHaas.com And true to my initials, SHhhh... I'll let it be our little secret.

More by Sylvie Haas

All books can be found at SylvieHaas.com

Claimed by my Ex's Dad & His Friend

Claimed by my Stepbrothers

Heat Stroked

Claimed by my Boss & His Twin

Claimed by my Best Friend's Brothers

Claimed by my Lawyers

And other sexy series!

Sylvie Haas Freebies

Do you love bonus content?

Sign up for my newsletter and you'll get access to all of my freebies, and I'll keep you up to date on all of my new releases and special offers.

https://SylvieHaas.com

About the Author

Why Choose one hero when you deserve them all!

Sylvie Haas obsesses over dirty-talking heroes who fall hard and fast for the woman of their dreams.

On most days, you can find Sylvie with the wind in her hair, her fingers on the keyboard, and her mind in the gutter as she thinks up new places her characters can get frisky.

Sylvie Haas is the pen name of a USA Today Bestselling author who's been a finalist in multiple romance writing competitions and has been asked to present internationally on writing short stories and novellas.

Sylvie's books are short, age gap, ménage and reverse harem romances, that will satisfy you with a light and fun happily ever after!

Find your next set of book boyfriends at https://SylvieHaas.com

Made in the USA
Columbia, SC
07 April 2024